THE FIFTH WOMAN

THE
FIFTH
WOMAN

NONA CASPERS

SARABANDE BOOKS
Louisville, KY

Library of Congress Cataloging-in-Publication Data
Names: Caspers, Nona, author.
Title: The fifth woman : a novel in stories / by Nona Caspers.
Description: First edition. | Louisville, KY : Sarabande Books, 2018
Identifiers: LCCN 2017039813 (print) | LCCN 2017033119 (e-book)
ISBN 9781946448170 (softcover : acid-free paper) | ISBN 9781946448187 (e-book)
Classification: LCC PS3553.A79523 A6 2018 (e-book)
LCC PS3553.A79523 (print) | DDC 813/.54—DC23
LC record available at https://lccn.loc.gov/2017039813

Cover design by Kristen Radtke.
Interior by Alban Fischer.
Manufactured in Canada.
This book is printed on acid-free paper.
Sarabande Books is a nonprofit literary organization.

  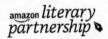

This project is supported in part by an award from the National Endowment for the
Arts. The Kentucky Arts Council, the state arts agency, supports Sarabande Books with
state tax dollars and federal funding from the National Endowment for the Arts.

FOR MY FAMILY AND FRIENDS
AND FOR MY LITTLE DOG COMPANION
OF FIFTEEN YEARS, EDGAR

On the roof of the house Geryon stood
looking out to sea. Chimneys and lines of laundry
    surrounded him on all sides.
Everything curiously quiet.

—ANNE CARSON, *Autobiography of Red*

CONTENTS

The *Fifth Woman* is stealthily astonishing from its first line to its last. Over the course of twenty-three connected short fictions of varying sizes and shapes, the writer marks out a trail of mourning that is both quite straightforward and miraculously layered, strange, and emotionally multifaceted. There is not a single sentence in these stories that is not as clear as water, but neither is there a single sentence here that doesn't, one way or another, cut deep. As I read and reread these stories, I tried to figure out how the writer cut to the bone with sentences like this. And how, I marveled, did the writer then build these sentences into stories of such power that, taken together, form a unified whole of such emotional depth?

I'm not sure I have the answers, besides sheer talent and

excellent craftsmanship, but I saw that the writer possesses what might be described as a transcendent honesty both physically and metaphysically. For example, the narrator, a young woman in San Francisco, remembers that her dead lover would "rifle through a drawer, her long fingers like antennae." This is love, this likening of the lover's long fingers not to, say, lilies, but to what they truly resembled when seeking. In another mode, the narrator remembers the exact quality of her lover's beauty: "She would be moving, and then she would be stopped, as if she had never been moving. And when she was moving, it seemed she always had been. Whatever she was doing took on the quality of the eternal." We mourn the lover with the narrator, but/and we mourn her precisely, specifically, and personally. She was *that* woman, that one who moved in just that way, a way that only someone who loved her deeply can share with us. What she did for a living or what brand of clothing she wore or how much money she made are only facts, and not especially relevant. They are demographics. But the "quality of the eternal" in the way she moved was hers alone, and the one closest to her is the one who saw it most urgently. The writer brings that sense of urgency to every word of *The Fifth Woman* and, generously, shares it with us with searching and scrupulous tenderness.

At one point in the collection, the narrator resolves to "write my own stories about everyday occurrences, like people reading things and thinking things, and stories in which the people and the animals just go on living the way we do, many of us, for a long time." Death, of course, is an everyday occurrence, one of the most everyday of occurrences, and with *The Fifth Woman*, the writer fulfills the narrator's ambition to dwell wholeheartedly in the impossible and heroic task of just going on living in the world as it is. It is a wonderful book.

—Stacey D'Erasmo, 2016

THE FIFTH WOMAN

ANTS

The book I'm reading belonged to my first lover, Michelle. At the top of one page, she has written her name and the date, then three dark arrows pointing down.

The line Michelle is pointing to says that it has not rained in Lima since 1940, but when I think about the statement it seems impossible. I read the line again, and yes, that is what the poet says. She must be making it up, but I think about the people waiting every day for the rain; they wait for the water to enliven everything, to make their world wet and green and soft.

An aberrant heavy cloud rests above my backyard. I can hear Larissa's contralto voice quaver through the screen door, off-key. She is inside the house cleaning. She makes up songs about her day, or the sky, or something she's noticed on our street.

The last time I saw Michelle, she was in the middle of the sidewalk outside our old apartment building, balancing on one leg and waving at me. I was already walking down the street away from her. I was walking briskly, happily, thinking about the unexpected November sun and feeling my body move down the street, the concrete under my tennis shoes, the air made even more pleasant by the smell of renegade fall jasmine and ferns from our neighbor's garden. The sun blew straight at me, and I had to squint through a yellowish haze. There was a moment of blindness, and then I created a frame of darkness all around me, as if I were looking through binoculars. There was a slight change in temperature, a shift in light; the air pressed against my forehead. Michelle called my name, or I turned, sensing something, and then she called my name. She stood on one leg. She was waving.

Earlier that morning we had been counting the ants on the kitchen table. November rains had been making the cold air damp and, until the sun appeared that day, no one had wanted to be outside except for the hard-core bicyclers, like Michelle, and the newly transplanted or visiting Northerners whom you could see wearing short sleeves in the park. Above the table a large window opened to the neighbors' pastel houses, their palm trees, the sky. We lived on the first floor of a four-unit building, in a one bedroom with a large kitchen/living room; the couch and the table stared at each other across an expanse of red and orange, a rug we'd found at Thrift Mart.

The ants had arrived with the rains, only a few, scattered on the windowsill, trekking up and down the frame, a reckless band of nomads. "Ants," Michelle had said that first day, staring at the windowsill as if she'd forgotten ants existed. She stood with her foot on a chair like she often did, her hands wrapped around her cereal bowl, drinking her leftover milk. The next day there were considerably more of them and they had traveled to the table. The table leaf on one side was stuck upright and we often forgot to clean thoroughly in the crack. Those first two mornings Michelle washed up the ants, I think, but then it rained again at night and the next day there were more.

The ants on the table that last morning had formed a long line from end to end. On my way to the bathroom I had glanced over and there the ants were, glistening in the sunlight, which was already unusually strong. Now, we watched a stream of them that appeared to be running in a continuous loop over and under the table. Michelle was watching from one side and I was sitting across from her watching from the other side.

"This has become a problem," she said.

"I don't know," I said. From my angle, the ants appeared as a glint of black, and then a black moving line, bulbous bodies perfectly tuned to each other, a crazy black ribbon as if they were wrapping the table as our gift. "They're not hurting any-thing. Seems like they're pretty happy."

"Happy?"

"Well, you know."

She got up and went to the sink and drank a glass of water. Michelle tried very hard to drink as many glasses of water as she could during the day, and she tried very hard to get me to drink as many glasses of water as I could, because we had read articles about how people who drank water lived longer and had more resilient skin and inner organs. Nevertheless, our hearts were not in it—we'd forget that water had anything to do with us, and then one of us would get a headache or feel inexplicably funny and the other would say, usually Michelle to me, have you been drinking water?

After Michelle drank the water she burped, and patted her chest as if she were her own baby. She tied a gold ribbon, left over from last year's Christmas wrapping, around the bottom of her jeans so they wouldn't get caught in her bike spokes, and while she did this I looked down at the top of her head, a mop of black hair, and I thought, *Michelle is a mop of hair.*

I remember that thought, but I can't remember what we did about the ants that morning. I can't remember if we washed off the table before we left, or if, when I got home from the hospital and then the morgue later in the day, I washed them off. Had they gone of their own volition?

We had moved to that apartment building in the City two years earlier from the northern Midwest; our neighborhood was in a district that averaged an annual 185 sunny days, though there are many more sunny days in other districts. Of those days only half start out sunny, and very few of them are in November. The City gets twenty inches of rain annually, and 90 percent of those inches in November through March. But it was fog, which sometimes posed convincingly as rain, that blocked the sun more often. We did not know anything about fog when we moved to that part of the City; when we moved to the City we believed that most days were sunny and pleasantly cool everywhere.

But even in our foggy district the weather was benevolent and supportive, compared to the violence of the weather in the Midwest. We could bicycle to the park in our jackets. We could walk outside most any time without thinking seriously about the heat or the cold, the way we were used to thinking about heat and cold, the way heat and cold can form a solid mass at the center of your thinking and then explode. We never listened to the weather reports and forgot for the most part that there was any weather, except for on those few really cold, damp days.

One neighbor in the building Michelle didn't like. She had appeared early on, outside the building with her girlfriend. A few months later we saw her walking up the stairs without the girlfriend and down the hall past the landlord's flat. She was a young art major studying somewhere in the City and had a tattoo around her very thin neck, a single thin black decapitation line. She was Chinese, like the landlord, and spoke elegantly in English with almost no accent, but she was quiet and we were quiet and unsure about whom we could talk to or who wanted to be left alone. She never made eye contact; she often wore a sweatshirt with the hood pulled up and her black hair fell over her eyes. "I don't like her," Michelle said once, which took me by surprise. We were dining on bowls of parsley, pea greens, and carrot tops, because the local market had had a sale and we were Midwesterners and sick of eating regular salads.

"You don't know her," I said.

"That's true," she said. "I don't know her and I don't like her."

I fell silent. The light in the room was artificial; the windows were black and it was raining. What a wind bellowed outside! And what a great job the windows did keeping the wind and rain out. That apartment did a great job at many things, but was expensive for two midtwenties women with mediocre-paying jobs, which is why we stayed home a lot.

"I'll tell you why," Michelle continued. "I don't trust people who wear hoods or floppy hats."

I can see now that Michelle probably wanted me to fight with her, something I hadn't done for a long time, perhaps because I had grown tired of it or perhaps the weather had made me complacent. I chewed on a carrot top and set down my bowl. "People hide for a reason," I said. "Your favorite poet hid in her bedroom and drawing rooms."

"I may not have liked her," Michelle said, "in person."

Later that evening, Michelle and I pretended the rug was a lake or a pool and we were synchronized swimmers. Michelle had performed on a high school synchronized swimming team called the Aqua Belles. She put on music, classical, and we got into position and pointed our toes and tucked into a tub or a half tub. We rolled onto our backs and shimmied in opposite directions; we linked our feet above us in a bridge and then dropped dramatically under the imaginary surface.

"I think," Michelle said, after we'd climbed into bed and kissed goodnight, "when we're old, we'll be together."

"I can't even imagine being old," I said, though I wish I hadn't.

She was a confident chewer. Sometimes her confidence and strong opinions made her seem arrogant or foolish, and other times they made her seem large, like a sun or meteor or a boulder on a green hill, or an acacia in full bloom off the highway. She was good with maps. She knew how to sew. She was a sultry kisser. In the night, she'd reach over and rest her hand on the top of my head, sometimes give it a little shake.

What did she want from me? What are the things that matter?

Just before the arrival of the ants, we had put a note under the door of the building manager, Ronald Chang, asking if we could have a new refrigerator. He wrote back the following:

Girls. Not broke, don't fix.

Another time he left this note:

Girls. Someone coming. Pipes.

Another time:

This is clean bug day, girls. Under sink.

We pinned the notes to our refrigerator, which was not broken but was old and small and refused to freeze ice cream.

Ronald Chang lived above us. He had grown up in Shenyang, migrated to the City twenty years earlier, and worked at the Golden Lotus in Chinatown. Was he the owner of the restaurant? We could hear him going in and out of his apartment and up and down the stairs. We could hear his television and his conversations in Cantonese on the telephone. When he saw us he smiled and said hello very loudly, as if he had to speak English at a forceful volume if we were to understand. We often had the feeling that we were not real to him, the way you feel when you are visiting another country. The inhabitants are a little fake, and you think you can do or say whatever you want because you are more or less on a stage set. But, fortunately or unfortunately, he also was not all the way real to us. It took years before the City lived in my bones and I could see myself as a fellow member, a citizen of the City.

Some things I can't remember. I can't remember if we had plants in that apartment, or if Michelle liked houseplants. I can't remember the exact sound of her voice, or where she parted her hair, or what she smelled like. I can remember the bike she rode, a ten-speed Cannondale, yellow, and how she brushed her teeth with baking soda and once used a wet wipe to damp down her hair when we were biking and it was falling in her face.

"Someday I'll have my own woodworking business," she said once, and then a week later pondered going to medical school. The second year we lived in the apartment, while she was working construction full time, she signed up for French, astronomy, and pottery classes.

"How are you going to do all that?" I asked.

"I don't know," she sighed. A week later she had to drop all three.

She was a dreamer. She was egotistical, romantic, manipulative. I loved her.

In the vacant houses where she helped build kitchen cabinets and lay wooden floors, she often found odd items, like the poetry book with the three arrows pointing down to no rain in Lima since 1940. She would show these items to me and collect them in our large living room closet. The day she told me she didn't like the neighbor, she had found a long thin piece of wood on which someone had written in black pen:

> This is your leg, I love
> Your lips, a dove
> One shoe
> One rack of lamb for you
> Two turtle gloves

Etc. all down the wood.

From the same construction site she had already brought home a black leather wallet left behind inside a drawer. A horse head was embossed on the front flap. Someone had left a note in the wallet, written in navy blue eyeliner.

To Jim: I hereby solemnly and gratefully swear to pay back every penny of the $600 I owe you. Have a nice day. Lisa.

Lisa had drawn a symbol next to her name and we couldn't agree on what it signified. I thought it was a special kind of stylized letter *M. Lisa M.* But Michelle saw an unclosed heart.

After we disagreed about the wallet, we went to bed and pretended we were sexual strangers. Michelle pulled the sheet over her head, and I could see her breath tent and cave. "What color are my eyelashes?" she asked, which is the kind of question she often asked in the middle of the night. "Michelle, brown. They're brown. Now go to sleep," I said.

But they were red brown, like the bark on cedar trees, like California redwoods.

There is something that happens when you live in a nice apartment in a pleasant neighborhood in my city, even in the less sunny neighborhoods. Especially if you grew up queer in an inhospitable place, though you may not have recognized the margins until you left. You start to feel as if you exist in your own separate country—the City is almost an island—and you can do whatever you want whenever and wherever you want. You start to feel as if, for example, you might be able to fly off the ocean cliffs without a glider, or that you could live solely on sprouts and carrot tops, or that you could careen down the hills on your bicycle without a helmet during rush hour. You start to feel, even though you know the feeling is not true and that the laws of the physical universe have not been altered just for you because you live in this fabulous city in this nice apartment, that you cannot be touched by normal human tragedy.

The evening before the ants arrived, someone knocked at our door. The neighbor Michelle didn't like had lost her rat. We went to help her find it, trolling up and down the stairs and hallway to her apartment, and then down into the basement and laundry room. We went up and down the street. It had misted most of the day and in the dim evening light the street and sidewalk looked black and oily.

"Hey, what color is your rat?" Michelle suddenly asked.

It struck me that she often asked questions I never thought to ask. I had assumed the rat was white and so I had been looking for a white one, but what if the neighbor's rat was brown or black? I thought it odd that we hadn't asked before.

"White," the neighbor said.

"What's its name?" Michelle asked.

"Whitey," the neighbor said.

She was quite beautiful, despite decapitation, with bright black eyes and wide, friendly cheekbones.

"Whitey," Michelle started calling. "Whitey, Whitey, Whitey."

There was a certain kind of sadness in her voice; I could hear the sadness even though she was loud, which she could be in public; the sadness seemed to drift over the streets and vanish. We circled the building searching in all the interstitial spaces, tamping down the damp weeds and coarse grass beneath stairwells and between buildings with our shoes.

After searching for a long time Michelle threw from her pocket into the street a rock she had collected at her work site. "The rat's dead," she said too loudly. I saw the young woman pull her hood further over her face. I remember feeling embarrassed, and angry, not because Michelle was rude, necessarily, but because she felt so at ease saying what we all thought. I felt I had to resist her somehow.

"Rats are resilient," I said. "They've lived in worse situations."

Michelle clamped her hands over her ears as if she couldn't bear my point of view, something I'd only seen her do a few times. "Dead dead dead," she shouted, and stomped off back toward the apartment.

Before she reached the door, she turned around and looked for me. I remember thinking, for a moment, that I would go inside. But then I turned away. Maybe I was still angry, or maybe I felt sorry for the neighbor, or maybe I wanted to prove something to Michelle. But I stayed outside searching for the rat for another hour. Then I sat on our front steps in the dark with the beautiful neighbor in silence. I might have put my hand on the back of her neck.

When I finally went inside the apartment, Michelle was not in the kitchen or in our bedroom or living room.

Then I heard a sound in the bathroom—it wasn't a sound

I had heard very often in the three years we were together, maybe a few times. Michelle was crying. In a minute she washed her face, and came out of the bathroom, and climbed into bed. Suddenly I didn't feel angry. And even though I didn't understand, I put my arms around her, and I whispered in her ear, "If you ever get lost, I'll find you, Michelle. My little Whitey."

That last morning I was a block away. The morning sun and air fell on my shoes, my arms, my face. The concrete glistened. Our neighbors at the end of the block grew jasmine and ferns in front of their house. That street was full of trees, and flowers planted around the trees, and people spraying Maxsea fertilizer. My work was only four blocks away, across the park, and I never had to hurry.

Michelle was carrying her orange helmet because she had left her bicycle at the site and planned to ride home early and make us dinner—I remember seeing orange. She yelled, "Don't forget to buy cinnamon!" For months we would put cinnamon on our toast, and then for months we would have no cinnamon. We would look and look and then we would say, "Someone needs to buy cinnamon." And then we'd forget. I did most of the grocery shopping.

Michelle was standing on one leg, clowning, or was she showing off? She looked so solidly there—she looked bound to the concrete: her rangy hips and low-slung work jeans and T-shirt. Her brown round arms.

The ants were winding their ribbons around the table or were washed up under our sponge and drowning in the kitchen sink.

When I arrived at work, the boss was out ill and the phones were ringing and ringing. Between calls I sat in my office chair and typed and edited several articles and letters. At three o'clock, exactly at three, the phones suddenly quieted. I looked at the clock, and then I looked out at the trees and the shadows moving over the trees. I didn't have much thought, or the thoughts I was having were buried deep in those trees.

At 3:15 the phone in my office rang. I picked it up and heard our neighbor the art major's voice. She has found her rat, I thought, and for a moment I ballooned with gladness for her. What a feeling that must be, to find a lost animal, even a rat, that you had loved and cared for daily and then suddenly lost and thought vanished forever.

She spoke very slowly and carefully, measured and loud, the way the landlord did, as if she were afraid I would not hear her the first time and she would have to repeat the words and that would be unbearable.

"Your girlfriend is hurt," she said. "You come home now."

Very few people speak in direct imperatives, except on television commercials, and then the sentences are usually happily directing you to buy some product. I hung up the phone. I couldn't move. I sat in my office chair next to the phone for what felt like a long time but was probably only a few seconds.

———

As it turns out, the connection between rain and the appearance of ants in one's home is a myth. This I read in "House-Infesting Ants and Their Management." As a group, ants are the most difficult household pests to control, and treatment methods such as spraying ant trails can make the problem worse. The best solution, according to the article, is to keep your house meticulously clean so the ants have no resources. Ants are social insects, and when they find resources they release a chemical letting everyone know where to feast. Although most ants consume a wide variety of foods (they are omnivorous), certain species prefer some types of foods and some even change their preferences to the preferences of the homestead. Common ant species include the fire ant, carpenter ant, thief ant, odorous house ant, crazy ant, little black ant, tramp ant, pyramid ant, big-headed ant, acrobat ant, ghost ant.

The article said nothing about ants coming in from the rain or cold, or about the danger of ants, except those ants that sting or eat the wood, and of course no one wants ants to infest her food supply.

I wonder if I would remember anything about that day if Michelle were still alive. Or about the Chinese landlord and his notes, or the man we never saw. I wonder if I would remember the morning sun, the sidewalk, the jasmine and ferns, Michelle carrying her orange helmet. I wonder if I would remember the run home through the park, the beautiful play of light and shadow, the majesty of the eucalyptus trees, and the four pillars of sunlight that streamed through them from the top of the hill. I was running and breathless and then boom—four pillars of light, filled with dust and floating debris, appeared, and I ran through the momentary warmth and shimmer.

When I reached our street—it could not have taken me more than five minutes—I didn't have to ask any questions. There was a small crowd of pale, vibrant-looking people who must have been my neighbors, and then five or six police officers, and a man in a car weeping, and a paramedic who grabbed my arm as I pounded on the ambulance door just after they raised her into it on a hydraulic gurney. She was wrapped in a blue blanket so she would not get cold. Michelle died in the ambulance, and by the time I reached the hospital, was already heading for the morgue.

I believe the ants we had that November were odorous house ants. *Tapinoma sessile*. They live under stones or boards in walls or under floors. They eat sweets, meat, dairy products, seldom have swarming seasons, do not bite, do follow trails and are about one-eighth of an inch long. They resemble fire ants, but when crushed emit a pungent rotten coconut smell.

A trail of cinnamon on the windowsill and countertops will deter ants. Ants don't like cinnamon.

Someone told me that cinnamon also prevents high blood pressure and heart attacks; you should eat a spoonful of cinnamon every day.

After Michelle died, I knew I had to move out of the expensive apartment. I would sit on the sofa and stare at the table and out the window—I thought if I waited long enough in one sitting, the ants would return, and she might become undead. She had been a willful person. The air would be gray and solid, a gray wall of winter fog, and then suddenly Michelle would walk out of the fog, looking straight at me, smiling, exhausted, happily exhausted and almost home. Time might change its mind and go backward, just this once. We see it in movies. We read about it in the Bible. I had grown up on the story of Lazarus. Even if she were bloody and decayed, I would have welcomed her. Maybe she didn't know that.

My fingers went numb. Sometimes my lips also went numb.

The day was officially described as follows: sunny and calm with highs of seventy degrees and a twenty-degree drop in temperature in the evening. A perfect seventy degrees. No fog or wind— or at least, on the City weather reports for that day, no fog or wind was recorded.

TWO CLEAN THINGS

There is a kind of wailing that sounds like singing. It comes from the hollow parts of the skull, and from the roots of the hair, and even from the thumbnails.

I was living in a third-floor studio apartment on a block that was said to have had the highest crime rate in the City. Even on the third floor the landlord, who lived across the country, had placed bars on the windows. Some of the bolts attaching them to the building had rusted and broken, and so bars were missing here and there. Whenever I left the building, I wore an over-sized coat and knit watchman's cap with my hair shoved inside so you couldn't tell I was a young woman. There was an alley off one side that the tenants unironically called "toilet alley," and it was also useful for selling drugs and sex, dumping garbage, and occasionally, or so I had been told, for dying. I had moved into the apartment over the alley after Michelle died; I wanted to live alone—I wanted to be alone—and after three months of looking I realized a place with bars on the windows and stains on the carpet was all I could afford. Across the alley stood a rooming house. My apartment over the alley had one window that faced the alley, though I could see the main street from an angle, and for two hours on late afternoons the sun blasted through. Monday through Friday I walked up Market Street to my job and down Market Street from my job. On weekends I worked on my literature thesis. At night I ate at my table and read stories and listened to the alley people's bowels and moans and whispers. There were sounds that defied language, sounds I've never heard again.

There was a man I saw, most days, in the alley, in the morning as I walked out the front door and turned right toward Market Street. He was gone in the evening. He wore a buckskin jacket and his face was lobster red and pocked with deep marks that I could see even from a distance. "Good morning," he said cheerfully, every time he saw me pass. He was sitting against the building, usually, or leaning up against it. I said nothing, not because I didn't like him or had a particular attitude toward his presence there, but because the morning comes to me like a box of puzzle pieces without the box; it takes me until noon to construct any reasonable or recognizable landscape.

Some days, I would attempt language; I would lift my head

slightly and open my mouth. He seemed to understand. He would put up one hand. Once he said, "It's all right."

"Good morning," he said one morning after I'd lived there for a few months, and then he said, "Wait. Wait."

I stood on the street. A pair of men's underwear—so clean it must have fallen out of someone's laundry bag—lay crumpled to the left of my foot.

"Come here," he said. "Just come close enough so I can toss you something."

The day was so cool—usually I didn't notice things like that on my walk to work, but the stopping made me feel the coolness of the air. I pulled my watchman's cap down over my ears and backed up a few feet. The man crouched in the entrance of the alley, about ten feet away from me, his back against the brick. He had one watery gray eye, tender and whale-like. I was surprised to see that the other eye was missing, but I couldn't look long enough to create a memory and describe it now, except to say there was wrinkled skin where the eye should have been. How had I missed such an injury? Later, he would tell me he had a sister in Berkeley and cousins in the City who owned a gas station. When he was a kid and worked there, he became addicted to the fumes.

He sat up and threw something, and I instinctively reached for it. It was clean. A stuffed animal, a little donkey with gray haunches and a white belly. A name was stitched into the belly with red thread.

"Are you Russell?" I asked.

"No, I'm Zach."

There was a tree on that street, a fat happy ficus that blew and blew in the wind, and the sun rose from behind a building and cast the tree's shadow, a thick branch, over the man so suddenly. Then a big leaf cast over and covered his red nose and leaves rippled over his buckskin jacket and he looked at me with his one eye, squinting in the momentary sun.

"Thank you," I said.

He pulled his coat up over the back of his head, making it into a shelter, and the tree, that marvelous, oblivious beast of rubbery green leaves, grew fatter over the years and is still there.

THE DOG

E very day during the summer, at about three o'clock, a shadow shaped like a dog appeared on my writing table. It was a small dog; I could see the head, the two pointed ears, the fluffy tail. The dog sat across from me at the far end of the table and then slowly approached until it disappeared at six o'clock.

I couldn't locate where the dog came from; it seemed disconnected from the dark rooming house across the alley, from anything in all the inhabitants' bleak dusty windows. I know this lack of source makes the dog unreal, but the dog was as true and constant as anything else in my apartment. I waited for the dog to arrive, and when it did I would sit working on my thesis with the dog for company. But some days, the dog felt like a bad omen, a nomadic wraith, and on those days I felt as if my apartment had somehow detached from the center of things, and were floating somewhere to the left of anything that mattered. I suppose I could've experienced those days as freedom, but I didn't.

Other things appeared in that apartment over the alley. Once, returning from work, I found a piece of paper near an open window with a handwritten verse on it:

> The merrier we be
> The sunnier we see
> and blinded by the light
> becomes a melody

The writer had scratched out *melody* and written *tragedy*.

Another time, when cleaning, I found a multicolored rubber ball under the couch; a week later a child's sock, though there were no children in the building or in the rooming house next door. In fact, I don't remember seeing a single child the three years I lived there. The sock was lime green with a picture of a horse face over the toe; if you put your hand inside, the horse's face bloomed into three dimensions and stared at you under droopy lashes. Another time, nearer the end of my stay, the sudden smell of lilacs hit me as I walked through the door, again with no apparent source.

Some days, the dog appeared to be sitting up, alert; other days the dog's head hung low; still other days the dog seemed to be sleeping, its head resting on its small paws.

One day the dog appeared with only one ear. I didn't notice the missing ear immediately—it was only when I looked up a third time, during the middle of a long and arduous thought, that I saw the one ear clearly sticking up and the other ear gone. The next day half of its tail was missing, leaving a fluffy stump. The next day it seemed to be missing a paw.

That night, in my bed, I began to imagine the dog outside my apartment, roaming the streets and scavenging, sleeping in doorways or maybe in alleys. I lay awake worrying about the dog, but of course there was nothing I could do, and I knew the dog wasn't real, and that there were real dogs out there getting hurt and I should worry about them. Nonetheless, I worried about my shadow dog.

I woke in the morning late, took a shower, and read another book. At one o'clock I sat at my table and tried to write, but I couldn't concentrate. I began instead to think about the dog. I had read an article about dogfighting in the City, about gambling rings and people who stole dogs off the street and out of cars to use for these fights. I imagined a basement with concrete floors and oil stains and a walled arena surrounded with chairs, the men in T-shirts smoking and drinking whiskey. And I imagined my little shadow dog in a cage in the corner, sitting quietly, shaking.

That's where I had to stop; it was too sad.

I had imagined the dog in the worst situation, but I could just as easily have imagined it roaming through the park, sniffing eucalyptus leaves, sleeping under the trees and stars.

At three o'clock, the dog appeared with one ear, half a fluffy tail, all four paws intact, and a shorter snout. But it looked content, its head tilted slightly to one side. I was happy to see it. I said hello, and then I went back to work. Now the apartment was brighter; there was a glow in my small room as there always was when the dog appeared. Every time I looked up the little dog was there, in its own way steadfast. Just as the air began to thicken and prepare for dusk, the dog vanished, and I wondered what shape it would be in the next day, what it would be missing, or if it would appear at all.

What kind of suffering are we off to? What kind of joy?

THE PHONE CALL

Every few months, when I lived in the apartment over the alley, I called my mother. Always on a Saturday or Sunday afternoon, more often in the summer and on warmer days, when I was home from grocery shopping or had finished cleaning my two rooms. We talked about the weather where I lived and the weather where she lived, though the weather where I lived was often the same, sunny or foggy, or sunny post-fog, or sunny with wind. The weather where she lived was more dramatic so we talked about it a lot. Storms with lightning and thunder, sheets of snow, icy rains, winds that blew things down, like an apple tree in the backyard and a piece of gutter from the roof.

Once, when I called, she was soaking a frostbitten finger in tepid water. Another time she was out of breath from ripping up basement carpet that had molded due to humidity.

After the weather, we would talk about the people in the town, or the people living outside of town whom we both knew. Sometimes she told me sad stories about people I did not remember or perhaps had never met. I liked the sound of her voice, and I liked hearing the details of other people's lives, people wounded in hunting accidents or run over by farm machinery or their children run over or somehow damaged by farm machinery.

The stories were often harsh. But my mother told them gently. She always said, at the end, "Isn't that sad?" And she asked me to pray for so-and-so, and I said I would, even though I knew I wouldn't because I didn't know how. Sometimes I would stand in my living room and shut my eyes and say in my mind, *I wish you all the best,* or, *I wish you a good day.* If I was passing a church in the City, I would step inside and light a candle, or I would see a candle while seated at a table in a restaurant, and I would suddenly remember a story my mother had told me.

I was confused about what to ask for. Happiness seemed too large, given that they had lost limbs or children, or their children had lost limbs, or they had cancer. Once, in a church, I kneeled in front of a statue of some saint or other, the one with the little dog, and I folded my hands and said a Hail Mary.

About my life, in my little apartment in the City, I said very little. "How is your thesis going?" she asked several times. It was going well, I told her, it was always going well, and sometimes this was true, and sometimes it was almost true. More often it was not true.

One day, toward the end of my stay in the building, when the thesis was almost finished and had indeed gone well, though I didn't know that yet, I called her early on a Monday morning. Her voice sounded different, fainter, and further away. She sounded puzzled.

"Is this you?" she asked several times.

"Yes, of course it's me," I said.

"Are you OK?" she asked several times. "It's Monday morning, you have to go to work."

She was right about that.

I told her I was not OK, but then, at the sound of her breathing, I took it back and said I was kidding, I was just a little tired.

Her voice remained faint and far away. There was the sound of her house barring the wind and the sound of my two rooms cloistered in fog. And then, the beginning of an even longer silence.

THE GUN

I kept a gun in the bottom drawer of my dresser. The black metal barrel like a dog's snout. The chamber—which did move and could hold bullets—was empty. If Michelle had been alive, she would never have let me keep it. But, if she had been alive, this story never would have happened.

I found the gun while digging up a plant behind the rhodo-dendron grove in the park. I wanted to bring the plant—the one that bloomed purple flowers she had liked—into my apartment for company. The park was so big, and so many plants flourished there, including many of these unofficial plants, that I didn't think it would miss the one. I had brought a plastic bag with paper towels soaked in water tucked inside. I had excavated the roots and was ready to put them into the bag when the black metal of the gun glimmered up at me. Without really thinking about what I was doing, and even though I knew I should report the gun to the police, I plucked it out of the ground, unplugged the dirt from its barrel, wiped off the metal with my watchman's cap, and slipped it into my jacket pocket.

Home in my studio apartment above the alley, I laid the gun on a towel on my small writing table. The plant fit nicely into a clay pot I had found in the alley some time earlier. I put the plant on the table next to the gun.

That night I went to the movies. In the movie I saw, Gregory so desperately loves Clara he can see no other way to be with her but to shoot her husband; the dead man's blood trickles out from his chest onto the kitchen floor like a red string. *They will never be happy,* I thought. Yet, in the next scene, Gregory and Clara are holding hands outside a hut in the mountains of Chiapas. They cook over fire and are teaching children to read. Clara cuts her hair and wears bandannas; Gregory tans an earthy brown and grows a beard.

I wanted the movie to end with them building a school or something, but of course they are caught. In the final scene Clara sits under a thatched canopy reading a book. A shadow of a figure blocks the light and darkens her back; her bandanna is askew; she delicately straightens it, and turns. The music imitates a heartbeat to tell us that she has been waiting for this ending. Gregory is walking down a hill toward her, in time with the music. He slows—surprise and then recognition. The camera zooms in to his face, which looks nothing like the face of the desperate lover with the gun in the beginning of the movie.

The movie ends.

When Michelle's cousin finally answered my knock she was wearing a robe made out of quilts.

"Michelle had a robe like that," I said.

She looked at me. I wanted her to invite me in, to offer me something to drink. She had moved to the City in spring and now it was summer and we hadn't seen each other since the funeral.

I stood at the door waiting.

She told me she couldn't let me in because she hadn't fully unpacked or cleaned her house. "The dust," she said. "The clutter." As soon as she spoke, I knew why I was there—they had the same voice, deep and solid as tree bark.

I told her I didn't mind dust or clutter, I would shut my eyes if she wanted me to, I would walk in backward, or she could blindfold me.

I unwrapped my wide pink scarf from around my neck and tied it around my head over my eyes. She laughed and let me in. Through the cotton fibers I could see pretty much everything, but I didn't tell her that. I sat at her kitchen table and fumbled for the glass of juice she set in front of me. I just wanted her to keep talking, but she didn't.

I told her about the movie.

"Why did Gregory have to kill the husband?" she asked. "You must be leaving something out."

I wasn't leaving anything out.

"Let me try again," I said.

I told her how every night, before they slept on the floor of their hut in each other's arms, Gregory and Clara hiked down a hill to a stream. I told her how the moonlight framed the white sand bottom, how the rocks gleamed like eggs nestled in moss. The water was clear and cold and smelled of mountain. But how soft, how soft the air and the stream and the light— how soft her skin submerged in darkness. Her lips were moss, stone, air. They kissed and kissed until they were too sleepy to kiss anymore.

As I spoke, my scarf scratched against my cheeks and my breath made the air warm inside, so warm I could feel my upper lip sweat.

Michelle's cousin was sitting back against her chair, her quilted robe wrapped carefully over her legs, which were thin, and nothing like Michelle's sturdy legs. Suddenly, the cousin leaned forward and stared at me, her face about six inches away. "In real life people let go of things they can't have," she said, gently. I nodded. She reached out and pulled the scarf free.

In the light of my small apartment the black gun shone, just where I'd left it, on the towel on the table, next to the stolen plant. It looked a lot like Gregory's gun, I thought.

I positioned my gun, finger poised against the trigger. I aimed the gun at the gray carpet and killed it. At the sofa and killed it. I killed the new plant with the purple flowers. I killed a few more objects in the room. My heart was a lost land, unreachable, barren, and cold. I pressed the gun to my chest and killed and killed each pulse that rattled there.

THE CLOSET

The carpet in the closet was beige and plush, different from the gray, flat carpet in the rest of the apartment. A few times, when the people in the alley were especially loud and I didn't want the company, I would slide my bedding across the living room floor and sleep in the closet, the door halfway open to let in a faint banner of light from the rooming house across the alley.

In that light I sat on the floor and looked through Michelle's things that lived in the closet, in a box on a shelf. Unanswered postcards from friends, her favorite jeans, her bandannas. Broken objects that she claimed she would fix: a hammer with a missing handle, a rotary telephone, a silver cigarette lighter shaped like a shark, a toaster without any trays to hold the toast.

Once, while sleeping in the closet, I woke from a dream that I was sleeping in the closet. It was the deepest sleep I had ever known, with the thud of horses galloping past.

RECEPTION

The Barbie doll legs were left by the previous reception-ist—tan, vinyl calves dangling over the edge of my desk. During the sixteen months I worked at CrackerBrokers Inc. I did not move them. The only other item on the desk was an old-fashioned beige telephone with three lines and an intercom. As soon as I saw the outmoded equipment, I knew this was the job I was looking for, and, indeed, the telephone rarely rang.

I sat at the desk reading books, or sorting out Michelle's mail. She hadn't accumulated a lot of obligations—a few bills, overdue student loans—the mail just kept coming. I told the senders Michelle was dead and wouldn't be making any more payments.

My desk faced a dark, wooden door in the entry of a suite on the top floor of a sixteen-floor building. The matching paneled walls were bare; there were no chairs or furniture, only the flat, soothing stretch of clean beige carpet. Except for Thursdays, the three brokers who had offices in the suite came and went all day; they answered their own cell phones and made their own calls. Behind closed doors the muted sounds of ring tones whirred, like distant birds in a vacant forest.

In those early days in the office, I moved as if my body were two halves stitched together. Days went on, zigzagging back and forth, from nothing to nothing. I have no idea why the broker on the phone had hired me, or why the three men kept me on. I don't even know why they thought they needed a receptionist.

My first morning on the job, I stepped off the elevator and one of my three new bosses, the one who hired me over the phone, greeted me. He wore a gray suit and an off-white shirt with a white collar. His name was Jim White. "I'm Jim," he said to me, and held out his hand, which was so fatty and soft for a moment I didn't want to let it go. He was about thirty pounds overweight and had a square head and fleshy nose that made me think of Captain Kangaroo. He walked me down a wide empty hallway, led me into suite 1601, and pointed to my desk. "Well, uh," he said. "That's your desk." Then he walked into his office and shut the door.

The other two brokers in the suite were named Carl and Ricky. Carl's was the first office off the hall and closest to my desk. When he left his office and walked by my desk he lifted one hand, which was proportionally large and reminded me of a Ping-Pong paddle, and when he returned he lifted the other hand. I said, in my most neutral voice, "You'll be going, then," when he left, and, "I trust you're well this morning," when he arrived. He lifted his hand as if he were waving, but also as if he were hiding his face, and then Carl walked down the hallway and into his office, shutting the door.

Ricky, the youngest, had a very loud laugh, pink lips, a tanned, gaunt face, and the narrow body of a serious runner, though I have no idea if he had ever run anywhere. He often dipped his fingers into white paper bags, pulling out bread, cookie pieces, chips, popping the food into his mouth and chewing amicably. To Ricky I said, "Ricky, good morning! Beautiful day!" And when he left to meet with clients I said, "Have a great meeting!"

The three bosses arrived and left according to their own schedules. They rarely conversed with each other, but they all spoke to me, even Carl spoke to me on occasion. They were all pleasant or pleasant enough. After the last boss left, I stuffed my hair under my watchman's cap, pulled on my coat, and packed up my bag. I was still carting Michelle's papers and old mail in a Safeway bag, but then I bought a backpack for the Safeway bag, plus my books.

Jim's comings and goings seemed the most erratic; maybe he was tuned to some primordial migration pattern. On rainy days he was buried in his office, sunny days he was in and out gathering clients, and when the fog hung thick outside his one window he appeared and disappeared with no apparent pattern, as if confused by the ambiguity. But he always called to let me know when he was arriving. In fact, in the sixteen months I worked at CrackerBrokers Inc., when the phone rang I assumed it would be Jim telling me his plans. "Don't expect me soon," he'd say. Or, "Long lunch." Or, "Not coming in."

Like everyone else, he wore suits—gray, blue, beige—but Jim wore his according to the day of the week. Sometimes his tie was in place, other times askew, and still other times his white shirt was unadorned, and he seemed naked compared to the other men. One sunny day he arrived with his shirt, coat, and tie in place and impeccably clean. But when he lumbered out for lunch with the client, his shirt was buttoned oddly, puckering at the waist, making him seem more like an untrained adolescent than a middle-aged, certified, and practiced food broker. To Jim I said, quietly, "Hey, Jim," or "Bye, Jim."

One Monday, during the middle of my tenure at CrackerBrokers Inc., Jim did not show up for work and did not call. I was reading a book about the old-world animals, those that roamed the continents and swam the seas but now don't live anywhere. I had flipped to the index and landed on the animals whose names began with *M*. I was reading these names over and over, subvocalizing the vowels and consonants. I was trying not to think about Michelle. In those days, I was often trying not to think about Michelle.

I was on *Martinique house wren*, when Carl walked by on his way to lunch and lifted his hand, a salutation and a shield. I said, "Nice lunch," and kept reading.

At *Merriam's elk*, Ricky stopped at my desk, plunging his fingers into a white bag. He plucked out a piece of something, maybe a doughnut, and popped it into his mouth. "What're you reading?"

I held up the book, which depicted a collage of a Tasmanian wolf, horned gopher, and giant shark.

"That gopher is eating a shark," he said, chewing. A crumb from the doughnut had stuck to his cheek, a cheek that used to have acne, and he had sharp front teeth, rather long like the horned gopher's. I imagined a shark eating Ricky.

"Do you think we have a chance?" he asked.

I knew he meant *we*, as in human beings on the planet Earth.

"Because, you know, this has been going on for a long time. This isn't new. I mean humans just pretty much wipe out everything they touch, don't they? It seems to me we're genetically flawed; I mean, maybe we deserve to die out, you know?"

It was difficult to ascertain if he meant what he was saying. I wanted him to go to lunch, so I could return to not thinking, reciting the names from my book, and staring at the door with its golden handle, as if it would open to a sunbaked cave, a verdant, sheltered meadow.

"You might be right," I said, the girl wearing her dead lover's watchman's cap. "But then I'm a destructivist."

He looked at me blankly, then he shrugged and walked out the door to lunch. I closed my book, pulled out my Safeway bag, and began shuffling through mail. I don't remember eating lunch those first six months in the office. If I had an appetite it was likely stuffed in one of the envelopes.

Every afternoon the mail person arrived. She opened the door and dropped the mail with a soft thump into a metal-wire receptacle on the floor. She appeared to be in her midtwenties, like me. Her black hair was slicked back in a ponytail that, as she tilted to drop the mail, slid over her shoulder; a bright gold necklace hugged the base of her neck like a glimmering string of lights. When she opened the door, I looked up, she looked at me and nodded, and I waved back, as if waving at an earlier self through the window of a moving train. She never stepped fully into the room, so I saw only her head, upper body, and arm. She wore something on her wrist, a band with a black symbol or word—it could have been a tattoo—and every day I strained to decipher it.

There was a certain kind of joy in the mail carrier's arrival and the mail thumping into the bin. I look up, she nods, I wave. I carry the mail to my desk and separate the envelopes into three piles. On the wall behind the desk were three mailboxes that the prior receptionist had labeled in bright red marker:

JIM   CARL   RICKY

I had surrounded the names with tiny ink dots, barely visible, so when you looked closely the letters seemed to float in a placid blue snowfall.

When I put Jim's pile into his box, I thought about how he hadn't called or shown up yet. In my first three months, Jim was the one who received the most mail, because he moved the most stock, as they said. Stock was big boxes of packaged crackers. The company carried fifty-six varieties of snack crackers, but only twenty-four were selling. Neither Jim, Carl, nor Ricky could seem to move any of the more aberrant stock, such as the chocolate-flavored cracker or the strawberry-and-milk cracker, though Ricky gave them as gifts to everyone he knew.

By Tuesday, Jim still hadn't shown up. I had just opened my book to *Montane hutia, a rodent in the Dominican Republic and Haiti*, when the telephone on my desk rang.

"Is Jim there?" a man asked.

I had assumed it would be Jim.

"Could I speak with him?" the man continued. He spoke in a low, unusually casual voice.

"Oh, I'm afraid not," I said. "Can I take a message?"

"Who is this?" the man asked. "Are you Jim's daughter?"

At first I couldn't decipher his words. But then I realized the man thought he had reached Jim's home; I had neglected to answer the phone with "Hello, CrackerBrokers," and his tone was an "I'm-calling-Jim-at-home" tone and had nothing to do with me or my life.

"Oh," I said, relieved. "I'm the receptionist. You called his office."

"Ohhhh," the man said, and he sounded relieved as well; his tone became more reserved. "Well, thank you very much. You must be very busy. I hope you have a nice evening."

"Thank you," I said. "And you have a nice evening also."

We hung up the phone and I felt pleased with myself. Though I had made a mistake, I felt that correcting it was one of the most useful things I had done for weeks. When I went back to the list in my book, I read through the *M*s and even beyond. Ricky left at the *Pig-footed bandicoot*, and then I left and locked the door.

Wednesday, Jim did not arrive and did not call, nor did he call the next day, which was Thursday, the day they met at the round table to the side of my desk to write up their sales activities and pool their numbers to report to some central office in the Midwest. (I never understood why Thursday and not Friday, but I wasn't curious enough to ask.) I tried Jim's cell phone but no one answered. A half hour later I called again, and then every half hour until lunch. The first few times I left this message: "Jim, this is the office, please call, OK?" Then I started saying, "Jim, are you OK? We haven't heard anything. Just call." Next, I said, "Jim, we're all worried about you. OK, please call. OK?" Finally I said nothing.

At noon, Carl came out of his office and instead of walking past, he stopped and picked up the doll legs and balanced them on his palm. It was the first and only time I saw him do that.

"Jim didn't call?" he asked.

"Not yet," I said.

Carl's mouth had little flesh flaps on either side, I now noticed, more pronounced because he was grimacing, or was he shoving his bottom lip up into his top? The flaps fell down over the corners and so made his mouth look like the mouth of one of the extinct prehistoric fish I had read about in my book. The *Deepwater cisco*.

"Mmm. Have you called his cell phone?"

"Several times," I said.

"Well, call again," Carl said. This was the first time Carl had given me an assignment, and, though I didn't call again, I felt delightfully surprised at having such a definite role. He put the doll legs down in the exact position on the corner of my desk where he had found them.

A few minutes later Ricky came out. He was not toting a bag of food and he was not laughing; in fact, he came charging down the hall from his office and stopped abruptly at my desk, head down. "What are we going to do?" he asked me.

"Do?" I asked.

"They're gonna call us," he said. "What do we say?"

"I don't know," I said. "Couldn't we just say Jim's been sick this week?"

"They don't care about Jim. It's the numbers. We add up the numbers, three numbers, and we won't have enough."

I had never seen Ricky look worried or hassled before. As he spoke, he absently fit his thumb over the doll's hollow lower waist, as if his thumb pad were a lid.

"I think you have to just give the numbers you have. They'll understand," I said. "It hasn't happened before. Surely there is some room to be human." I thought of Michelle, gliding down the street outside our old apartment building, happy, no bicycle helmet. Then I thought about the man in the car, the driver who had hit her, weeping—innocent—and my own feral sleepless nights. I looked back up and saw that Ricky was anxiously watching me.

He stood up straight, relaxed his shoulders, removed his finger from the doll's legs, and laughed. "Oh, heck," he said. "It's just one week. What's a week!"

I was surprised that I cared. But suddenly I did care.

"Yeah, just one week," I said. "Jim will be in tomorrow."

On Friday I started thinking we should be calling someone besides Jim. Shouldn't we call his daughter? "Jim has a daughter?" they asked. Ricky and Carl rang his cell phone several more times, but no one answered, and then the voicemail was full. I searched the drawers of my desk for other contact information; I had really opened only one drawer before, the top drawer, which held the usual pens, Post-its, a telephone directory, a half pack of mint Life Savers. In the bottom drawer I found the other half of the doll, with dyed-pink hair and pink lips. Pulled over her busty torso was a red tube top. For a moment, I thought about joining her top half with her bottom half, but she looked so serene I decided against it, and placed the top half back in the bottom drawer.

———

Monday morning, I couldn't get myself out of bed. I had spent all weekend thinking about a world without all those animals, and then I thought about the emptiness of my world, and in thinking about this I got to work late. Ricky and Carl were already ensconced in their offices. I sat at my desk and stared at the door for a while.

I was standing by the watercooler when the elevator down the hall opened and Jim stepped out. I was sure it was Jim with his slouched shoulders and large head. He was wearing sunglasses and his beige suit, his Wednesday suit, but this was Monday. I was about to call out, "Hey, Jim!" But instead of walking toward our suite, he walked in the opposite direction and turned right down a hallway leading to the north end of the building. I followed Jim, walking quietly about twenty feet behind him. He looked different that day; perhaps it was the way he was carrying his upper body, a lighter step, his shoulders and head seemed to float. I looked down and thought about what was missing: shoes. I thought the word *shoes* and then I thought the word *socks*, but he was wearing socks. Black socks. As he walked I could see the heels and soles picking up lint and debris from the carpet.

I followed him around a corner and then, at the very end of the hall, I saw him open a door and step inside. I stood outside the door and pressed my ear against the dark wood, but I couldn't hear anything. A minute later a burst of deep laughter erupted from inside, and then a cough. I knew I should turn back, that whatever Jim was doing in the room was not my business. But, for the first time since I started working there, I could feel my curiosity pulling me forward, the whole weight of my mind toppled into the front of my skull, wanting to know, wanting to open the door.

As I opened the door, a bright light flashed into my eyes—so bright I had to close them and open them again. The room was crazy with fluorescent light reflecting off the bare white walls and ceiling. I stepped inside. I don't know how he managed it, but Jim was nowhere. Except for an abandoned metal desk facing the door, the room was empty. Perched on the desk was a green ceramic ashtray shaped like a duck; it held two cigarette butts. I touched the butts and they were cold.

I stood just inside the door, in front of the desk, with the duck and four walls and the gray carpet, which I noticed was stained with a circular splotch, strands radiating out from the center like sunrays. I bent down to touch the stain. And, as I bent down, out of the corner of my eye, I saw Jim's socked foot under the desk. I saw Jim's socked foot, moving, and then I saw the hem of his pants resting against his pale lower shin. He had either climbed under the desk when he heard me, or he was already under the desk before I stepped inside. His back was curled and facing me, and his beige pants stretched tight against his large, vulnerable bottom. Resting on his folded hands, as though he were sleeping, was his pink, lumpy face.

I don't know how long I was crouched there. I listened to my own loud breathing and Jim's softer breathing until the whole room vibrated, the skin on my hands and neck tingled, and for a moment I lost track of where or who I was. What was I doing here? Not just in that room with Jim, or in that suite behind that desk, or in my apartment above the alley, but what was I doing *here*—in existence? I looked at my hand, and forearm, and elbow. I looked at my fingernails and how the skin of my fingertips rose above them like little pink hills. I felt my cheek, the bones around my eye sockets, my wispy eyebrows. Whoever I was inside this sack of skin, I could feel my story vanishing into the brightness of the room.

After a while, Jim spoke in a voice I could barely hear. He sounded as if he were calling from very far away, a distant meadow, a cave, a forest. "Don't expect me today," he said. "Or tomorrow."

The rest of the week I called in sick and lay on my couch thinking about Jim. I thought about him in the morning when I awakened to the sounds of the alley outside my apartment window, midday when I went grocery shopping, and at night when I sat on the couch reading. The paleness of his shin, his linty socks, the blue vein struggling out of his collar. After that day I found him under the desk, he spent a month in the hospital on medical leave. Carl and Ricky sent him flowers and visited, to my surprise, but I never went. His back had gone out, the story was.

Before I left CrackerBrokers Inc., I finished reading the book about extinct animals and started reading about the ones that were not yet extinct but were about to be, like the polar bear. Do you know polar bears can hear a seal breathe under

THE CAT

We called her in our minds The Cat. The cat belonged to no one and everyone in the apartment building, though we never spoke about her—only later we did. Her bowl and water dish sat near the stairs in the first-floor lobby. If the bowl was empty, we put food in it; if her water dish was empty, one of us filled it. The cat was black, but not strictly black— when she lay in the sunlight one could see a maroon sheen. The cat was maroon and marooned. She didn't seem to mind; she lay around on the hall carpet, rubbed against our banisters, doors, and legs, sprinted up and down the stairs. She never complained vocally. She stayed mostly on the top two floors with forays to the first floor. Once, early on, she came inside my apartment, but only after I coaxed her with tuna. (Later I learned nearly all the occupants had coaxed her inside their apartments at one time or another.) She sat next to me on my sofa while I stared out the window for a few hours, and then I stopped, and she pawed the door, and I let her out.

Sometimes in the morning when I opened my door, the cat was waiting outside; she escorted me out of the building. And when I came home, she escorted me back up the stairs.

On my last day in the building, everyone's final day, in the middle of the afternoon, about a month before the building was sold and torn down and replaced with a fancier building none of us could afford to live in, the cat began to meow. It started as regular meowing, but then grew louder. Homing in on a low note, trilling up and ending on a high one. Or starting high and ending low. Over and over, walking up and down the hallways. I went out for a burrito and came back and there was the meowing, even louder, like a kid who's discovered a new room in her throat. It went on into the evening. I heard doors opening occasionally and tenants mumbling. At nine o'clock I heard a door slam. Then the meowing moved to the basement, which muted the sound but made it more haunting.

It mixed with moaning from the alley; the moaning made a bass line and the cat's song rode up and down it. As if the aria were blessing the moan. The notes rang out into the alley and street and wafted in through our windows. They seeped through our walls. I tried to sleep, but I could hear things in the song: at first I heard a stream trickling down a mountain, then a young Bulgarian woman keening on a rock, then a train in the distance, a metal door opening, a factory assembly-line belt, a ship's whistle, a Cantonese folk song, a human cannonball shooting out from a cannon.

In the middle of the night it stopped.

I sat up in bed. For the first time since I'd moved in, all was quiet. None of the usual sounds in the hallways, no mumbling, no doors opening and closing. No rotted wood boards creaking (the building was slowly caving in).

The streetlight shone in through the window. In my bedroom, on the wall across from the foot of my bed, I saw a water stain I had never noticed before. A rusty bell shape with tendrils, like an upside-down jellyfish. I watched the bell contract and the mouth open and shut; I watched it glide across the wall, and I began to wonder what the people in other rooms were seeing. Were they awake and staring at their walls? I wondered what the world would look like the next morning, when we all woke up.

WEATHER

I t was a clear, sunny day, the sun so bright and insistent that
the air looked yellow and the brick building across the alley
glittered. But inside the air was cold. Something that looked like
ash was blowing in my half-opened window. White, diaphanous,
like tiny moths.

I pulled the comforter to my chin and watched the ash drift
above me. A thin coat of white was already piled on the blankets
and on the windowsill and on the living room table and gray
carpet. I opened my mouth—it tasted like snow.

I used to follow my father across the fields to the barns,
plowing through snowdrifts, my mittens insufficient against the
cold. The breath of cows rose like ghosts into the rafters as he

siphoned samples of milk from the tank. And then we'd tromp back out into the snow.

I got up and put on my warmest shirt and pants, and I put on my overcoat and watchman's cap. I couldn't find my scarf so I tied an old pair of flannel pajamas around my neck and face, immediately noticing the ice forming underneath my nose. "Condensation," I said out loud. In my closet I found my old brown shoes; onto my hands I pulled a pair of socks. I tromped back and forth across the living room, the whiteness sparkling up around my jeans, and then I tromped into the kitchen. The cupboards sat under two-inch drifts; fields of snow swelled across the toaster and on top of the refrigerator. I heated water and made myself hot chocolate and sat at my desk holding the warm cup in my socked hands, and wishing I had marshmallows. I felt a certain kind of calmness that accompanies numbness, and with that a certain kind of joy. The blood huddled in the center of my body, hollowing out my limbs. Calm and joyous and hollow. I held on to my cup, and took another sip, and looked out over the snow.

It was up to my knees. Thicker, whiter. I kicked a path toward the bedroom but the wind began to blow. I pulled my cap down to my eyes and tightened my makeshift scarf over my face and pitched into the wind. The snow bucked. At first I was excited, in the company of such character, but then I felt afraid. My bed was gone. My socks were blocks of ice. I burrowed toward the living room but the sofa and table were gone. The wind yeed and yawed.

————

The wind stopped. The air warmed, and wet clumps followed by balls of iridescent hail popped against my cap and coat like buckshot falling out of the ceiling. Then the hail melted into rain. I stood in the middle of my living room and bent my head back as if being anointed. The rain grew more ambitious. I sloshed to the closet for my slicker and rubber boots. Under the plastic roof of my hood I listened to the drubbing of the rain.

The thunder shouted something I couldn't decipher, then lightning performed, which I was happy to see after so many years in a reasonable climate. The room darkened, reminding me of a charcoal drawing I had made in seventh grade. My mother against my will taped it to the mudroom wall. The air smelled sulfurous like boiled eggs. I was hungry.

In the refrigerator sat a bottle of ketchup. My hood fell to the right and the rain pelted my nose and the rain trickled down the left side of my face, making a gulch of my inner ear, then spilled onto my neck. I thought about the roots of corn, hay, barley, and beans; the worms worming their way deeper into the earth, stirring up the nutrients in the soil; the pigs, cows, goats, sheep, horses, chickens, turkeys, rabbits, and humans eating the corn, hay, barley, and beans.

The clouds turned white and began to part. The sun came spanking shamelessly across my white walls and beige couch. Thank god, it gleamed across the red table and the windows.

What a clean smell arose then—a crackling clean smell,

mixed with the smell of my laundry detergent. I thought, *What a lovely day, now forever scented with lavender*.

The couch and the carpet and my bed were drying in the sun, gathering more and more heat. I put on my bathing suit. I lay in the sun on the gray carpet. First I lay on my back and felt my front bake, then I lay on my front and felt my back bake. I smelled grass and manure. I smelled insects and dandelions and wheat. I smelled hay and squirrels dead in my father's traps and the dank moss of lakes. The air grew hotter and hotter, and I started to sweat and my lungs felt laden and hot and wet and I couldn't think. My muscles sank like dead things against my bones.

The cows refused to come out of the barn. The dogs slinked into cellars. Mosquitoes sucked us raw and itchy.

I kneeled at the half-opened window, my eyes shut. An evening breeze blew in. My opened mouth and throat became a tunnel and the breeze drifted into the spaces between my organs and the cavity of my brain. Inside my cells, leaves began to fall.

I put on my dry jeans and shirt. I made myself a cup of tea. I sat on the couch with a book. The cows grazed up on the hill, the freezer was full of venison, and the ocean smelled of the blood and flesh of freshly butchered chickens.

A HAT SHAPED LIKE A DOG
THAT LOOKED LIKE A CAT

One morning, on my walk to work down Market Street, I met a friend who also was walking to work. He had been a friend of Michelle's mostly, but after her death, for a short while, he had become my friend.

We ate dinner together several times at my favorite taqueria. The last time, he had leaned forward in his chair and reached over his burrito to hold my hand. I couldn't look at him while he held my hand; instead I looked at his plaid shirtsleeve, or rather at the yellow threads which seemed to be unraveling.

The atmosphere was very quiet in this particular taqueria, but the workers, three men behind a glass counter, were loud, or at least two of them were. Often these two men, when they saw me, would meow because one winter, when Michelle was still alive, I had worn a hat shaped like a dog that looked, to them, like a cat.

That day on the street, my friend was not wearing his plaid shirt; in fact, he was not wearing anything I recognized from the past when he and Michelle, and sometimes the three of us, used to sit in cafés and drink things, or walk around the Castro, or when I'd had dinner with him alone those few times, over a year ago. He was wearing a gray-blue suit, and a white button-down shirt, and shiny black shoes. His hair was shorter, and his eyes were brown.

"Did you always have brown eyes?" I asked.

He said that his eyes had been hazel most of his life but they had gotten darker suddenly, and that the same thing had happened to his father at the same age, which was thirty-two. When my friend had gone in recently to renew his driver's license he put down that his eyes were hazel. But the man behind the counter said, "Your eyes are brown."

My friend said he had been waiting for his eyes to change color, and so he had taken a photograph of himself every day for the past year. He carried these in his briefcase. "You can see them changing," he said. And as we stood on the sidewalk flipping through all those photos, I could. He also said that as his eyes changed he stopped feeling like the same person. He no longer, for example, felt like a man who would wear tattered flannel shirts or a man with scruffy hair hanging over his neck. He was single when I knew him; now he was married and his wife was pregnant.

His story reminded me of the mole on my forehead. About two weeks after the funeral, I went into the bathroom and turned on the light. But the face in front of me looked different from the one I had remembered; I didn't recognize the shape or the color, the hue. The dark mole above my left eyebrow, which had been there since childhood, was gone. My face could just as easily have been someone else's, and somehow, this new face allowed me to go on.

"I'm happy for you," I finally said to my friend, and I reached out and held his hand. I had expected his skin now to be smoother, but it felt as rough as it had before, when we sat in the taqueria.

That night, on my walk home from work, the sidewalks were empty and the air had become foggy. Ahead of me, three trees I hadn't noticed before hung over the walkway, their thick curtain of slivery vines, their leaves golden. They were whispering something I could almost hear.

THINKING

I was walking in the park on an April afternoon, the sun slanting through the branches and leaves toward my bare head. It was the first time since Michelle died that I was without my watchman's cap. Leaning forward, watching the space about three feet ahead of me, I pretended I was shooting a film. When I walked across the grass the screen filled with green, when I walked across the dirt it filled with the color of dirt, when I walked on concrete the screen was gray. I was trying not to think about the past. But also I was trying not to think about the future.

The park was full of people, in packs and dyads and solo. A family lounged on a pink blanket. The baby was crying, and then the baby stopped crying and started to laugh. Several people dashed by on Rollerblades, men and women, and several boys on skateboards. There were dogs. Big red dogs, small white dogs, and medium-sized tan dogs. I noticed that a lot of the tan dogs had shadowy markings around their ears.

Further into the park I hiked up a hill through thickening bushes and trees, then down the hill into a shady cavity. It was a small glade, carpeted in dark, golden leaves and fine sand, the kind of glade found in movies and books about gnomes, dwarves, and underworlds. I began to think something magical was going to happen. A radio played the news.

There was a laundry line about ten feet ahead of me, strung across the bottom of the glade; a pair of brown pants hung over the line. A stone shaped like an anvil served as a table for a coffee mug and a bright silver spoon. A few feet down the hill, I saw a green pup tent, and then I saw bare feet sticking out the opening. A thick book with a red cover lay on the ground next to the feet.

Here it is, I thought. *The gnome of the glade will have a message for me.*

Wouldn't you have waited?

On the other side of the hill, the sun was sharp and there was a cutting wind. Everyone was wearing sandals and had painted toenails. Blue toes then green toes then orange toes—how odd they looked, like flower bulbs or malformed carrots.

I read somewhere that without toes we would not have

learned to walk upright, but that even one toe, especially the big one, still would have made a huge evolutionary difference. In my shoes, now on the sidewalk, I lifted up my toes and took a few steps on my heels. It was awkward, but I believed I could keep walking this way.

Before I met Michelle, another woman had fallen in love with me. She stood in front of a window facing me; a blue sky framed her head and the sun infused her brown hair with light so I could see individual strands looping up and down like the tracks of a roller coaster.

"Will you marry me?" she asked.

I was standing about ten feet away, near the door, my jacket in hand.

"Yes, of course," I said, and we both laughed. We were never lovers. Two months after that she faded out of my life, or maybe just my memory.

We don't know where thoughts come from. The scientists have studied and studied, but we still don't really know why this one and not that one.

The park went on and on. There was a bee on a yellow rose petal, a green larva on the leaf of a rhododendron tree, and a long black something spilling from the grass to the sidewalk, which turned out to be a shoelace. Meadows filled with people eating food, but later in the day meadows emptied of people, and later still, when the evening sun made the tree trunks look like slate, a stream of cars and bicycles flowed toward home. To my left, in a fire pit, a single coal smoldered. I found a stick and buried the coal in hot ash.

The radio in the glade had been playing a story about the pole-vaulter famous for astonishing the athletic world not only for jumping so high but also for being the first person to catapult himself backward over the pole. "I didn't think about it," he said to the reporter. "I just jumped."

The woman who had fallen in love with me had eyebrows so faint that her forehead looked like the Great Plains, vast and open and fertile.

I remember hiking in those plains, gathering cow bones in an old blanket, wandering amidst the live cows and the tall grasses and the farmer's fields, pretending to be a heroine in a novel, worrying about how I ever would become someone worthy of the mystery of sorrow.

THE HORSE

I.

Every day for two years, I sat on the couch reading stories for my thesis, which was about animals, or rather about animals and place in contemporary literature. I was especially curious about the literary portrayal of North American farm animals. In one story, "Three Days" by Samantha Hunt, Beatrice and her younger brother decide to ride their old farm horse, Humbletonian, to the new mall complex a mile down the highway. They are drunk and it is freezing. The story mentions this several times. Beatrice and Clem saddle the horse, Humbletonian, and clomp off down the road uneventfully: they listen to *the click of Humbletonian's hooves and the rush of the horse's warm pulse*. When they reach the Middleland Mall, they tie the horse to a corral for carts outside Walmart, and then they go inside. But when they return, Humbletonian is gone. They search and search and then, a page later, behind Walmart, they discover at least twenty bulldozers and a gigantic hole: *It is tremendous, far larger than a football field, and it is filled with water.*

As soon as I read the sentence about the hole of water, I knew the horse was going to drown. I set the story down, and said out loud, "Oh no, the horse is going to drown." My chest tightened and I felt dread, and then an anticipatory sadness, and then dread again, though I can see now that my anxiety had begun paragraphs before, probably in the first paragraph where the protagonist is walking in darkness down the highway and passes a bloated dead raccoon.

When I set the story down, the first thing I did was look at the back of my hand. I looked at my hand with its blue veins and geography of lines that I had always liked. As I've grown older, the veins and tendons have become more pronounced, like mountain ridges on a topographical map. After I looked at my hand, I went into the bathroom and cleaned the sink, and then I cleaned the bathroom floor with a washcloth. I thought about cleaning under the tub; in fact, I did not clean under that tub until I moved out two years later. Then I was surprised that although the floor was dusty, it was really not that dirty.

After I cleaned the bathroom I didn't know what I wanted to do. I didn't want to clean anymore, and I didn't want to talk on the phone, and I didn't want to go outside. And even though I knew the horse was going to drown, I began to feel hopeful that, somehow, the story would veer in another direction; the brother and sister would save the horse or the horse would save itself.

I picked up the story again. Humbletonian has climbed down into the pit and is walking across the surface of the ice that has formed there. The storyteller speculates that one of the bulldozers broke a water pipe while digging. *There is a lot of water here, a reservoir's worth of drinking water, or, Beatrice hopes not, frozen sewage. Humbletonian is walking across the ice, bending every now and again to lick the surface. Gross.*

In the next paragraphs, we read about the silver beauty of the horse and the *gorgeous ice and dirt and the lovely darkness, thick like felt.* And in the final sentence of those paragraphs *a jealous hole cracks open* and swallows the back end of Humbletonian. She *tries to clear the water, to get a hoof back up on solid ice, but each clop of her front hooves shatters what she's grabbed and pulls it under with her.*

The reader, along with the sister and brother who are standing helplessly on the rim of the ice, watches the horse thrash in the cold water. And then the horse starts giving up. She falls still. *Beatrice can see a lot of white in the horse's eye, as though it had been pried open. It blinks dry air once more, for the last time. Humbletonian's head goes under and all Beatrice can see are her forelegs above the barrier of the ice. Her legs kick, emptying what's inside them. It is a gruesome convulsion.*

I sat on the couch. I could not even look at the back of my hand.

2.

After this, I walked into the bathroom again but then I just stood there. I couldn't remember what I was going to do. I could see the horse thrashing through the ice and the water closing over its eyes, which had gone white. I could feel the constriction of sadness across my chest and in my mind. I played the scene again and again, thinking I would get used to the outcome, or eventually would be able to see the horse more objectively, as a metaphor or symbol. But each time I felt the pang of unfairness, and each time I felt the fear of the animal and the stupidity of the sister and brother. They were drunk. It was freezing. The sister had moved off the farm to a big city a year earlier, and it had been her idea to take the horse to the shopping complex, probably to prove a point.

I went on with my day, but after a few hours I began to question the use of reading the story. I questioned the use of fiction in general—what did we gain?

I also felt bad about the stories I had glorified in my thesis in which characters die, even though they die for a good reason. I thought I did not want to write about those kinds of stories anymore; instead, I would write my own stories about everyday occurrences, like people reading things and thinking things, and stories in which the people and the animals just go on living the way we do, many of us, for a long time.

3.

A few more hours after reading the story I realized that I could stop some of my anxiety by telling myself the event did not happen. I could say, this story is not real, this did not happen, though of course I knew in another part of me that things like that do happen, that the story is in fact happening every day.

4.

After I wrote the previous paragraph I thought it should be the end, but then I thought, *This isn't what I came to say either, is it?*

5.

My friend Kris has a horse with a beautiful white mane and coat with burgundy splotches, and he has amber eyes that glow in the darkness of the barn like the eyes of barn owls. Once, when I was visiting her in Minnesota, she told me that animals do not suffer or feel pain the way humans do, and she accused me of overidentifying with and even personifying animals. She said this because I had just told her a story about my brother's dog.

Two summers ago, my brother's nanny left his two-year-old golden retriever in the back of his SUV after a lake outing. She had unpacked the kids and bags of lake stuff, but she forgot about the dog. It was a hot day. When my brother found his dead dog he discovered that it had chewed off all the door handles.

Can you see it gutted?

My friend was right about my overidentification with

animals; it was one of the reasons I was having a hard time writing my thesis, but also one of the reasons I had chosen the topic. She was not right about my personifying animals. I do not think animals are humans nor do I want animals to be like humans. What I love about animals is that they are not human, but I do feel bad that humans, including myself, have ruined so many things for animals. Even a cow knows when to stop eating grass from a worn-out hill.

6.

I ended up going for a walk through the City, but I couldn't get the horse off my mind. The white eyeballs, the front hooves in the air crashing down on the ice, the gruesome final convulsion. I couldn't get the idea out of my mind that the sister and brother could have done something to save the horse. I called my friend Kris on my new cell phone and told her the story, and even though she thought I was overreacting, she agreed that the horse could possibly have been saved.

We talked about the story, and about the baby coyote Kris had seen two weeks earlier on a bluff in southeastern Minnesota.

7.

When I am old I will walk and walk through the woods and meadows of North America. I will not bring a camera or notebook, only my eyes, my ears, my nose, and my skin. I will sleep near streams and hike up mountains. The sun will bake my skin brown and my hair white and I will hobble like an old mountain goat. Give me my green green grass and blue water. Give me my mineral-flavored air and rain to wash the dirt off my hooves.

On my way home from my walk, I lay on a hill in a park and stared at the tops of eucalyptus, cypress, giant sequoia, redwood, madrone. I listened to the earth's dense whisper and the air's silence; all the birds were cooing or cawing. A dragonfly landed in the crease of my neck.

8.

As soon as Beatrice sees Humbletonian on the ice she runs into the store. Everything is happening in slow motion, but she keeps on going. She rallies the Walmart workers in their blue aprons that say WALMART, HOW CAN I HELP YOU? Someone from Yard and Garden grabs a rope and someone in the candy department grabs a caramel apple and at least twenty Walmart workers follow Beatrice out the back door. The cashier from register three knows a lot about ropes and horses and she instructs the sister and brother to say encouraging things while holding out the apple: "Listen to me, Humbletonian," Beatrice says. "We're going to get you out. Don't give up. You're just resting for a moment." And that's when the woman tosses the rope over the horse's neck and slips it under her front legs and yells, "NOW!" The bulldozer inches forward and all the people line up along the rope and everyone pulls and pulls and pulls and their hearts race and they feel their determination like a beast, like a beast, and together they pull the goddamn horse free.

THE FIFTH WOMAN

It was Sunday, and in the alley outside my apartment there was a party. Four women and one man were drinking from a brown bag. I watched them from my writing table, through my fingers like a mask. Earlier I had been watching them through my scarf fringe, and before that I watched them without anything between us. I imagined them as some kind of family.

They had begun in the morning and it was now mid-afternoon. Each stood in her or his original morning spot. The women formed a half moon around the man, who leaned against the wall of the rooming house across from my building. The man was tall, unusually tall, and his hair was longer in the front than the back and dangled into the emptiness of their half moon. At one point the man left, but then he returned a short while later, and stood in his same spot, with a large bag of Cheetos.

The women were shorter, even the two very tall women, and larger on the top than on the bottom, with barrel chests and narrow hips and skinny legs. They all had dark straight hair and they all wore jeans and colorful shirts.

One of the women wore a tight lime-green shirt that sculpted her fat into sections, her legs sticking out from the shirt in a way that made her look like a panda-shaped balloon. She rarely spoke but she opened and closed her mouth in silent laughs as she leaned back into the alley. Another woman wore a bright fuchsia T-shirt, and across her broad back spread a painted toucan. The toucan was saying something, its bill wide open in speech, but I couldn't read the words. The woman next to her had draped a piece of fabric or a blanket over her head and shoulders; every once in a while, as she spoke, her hands flew out, and the blanket slipped, and she readjusted it.

The hands of the blanketed woman were noteworthy, long and muscular. I began waiting for her hands to appear, and when they did, I leaned forward and thought about how she had achieved them. Michelle also had remarkable hands. I'd watch her rifle through a drawer, her long fingers like antennae. It was difficult for me to believe that her hands were dead.

That day, the apartment felt like a sanctuary. The sofa and the table kept me company. I felt them doing something like breathing; certainly they had a relationship with the air. The sofa looked very friendly in the artificial light. It said something, but I didn't know what, a tight sound. The carpet, which was gray and often morose, did not seem morose that day, though I would not call it cheery.

I walked into the kitchen and found on the bottom shelf of the refrigerator half a stuffed squash and a thick piece of cornbread. I had cooked the squash and baked the cornbread a few days earlier—but I had forgotten that, and so for a moment it felt as if someone had cooked a meal while I was at work, and left it for me. Or as if the apartment itself were taking care of me.

I sat on the sofa and ate the squash and bread. The party was still going on—maybe they were having a reunion. They had found each other again, in this city, in my alley.

Once, the voices flared up as if an argument was about to start, a fight. But a minute later they all started laughing, a lot of laughing in different tones and cadences. Some phrases I could understand: *high not, you know* and *electrical* something.

I watched them on and off into the evening, leaning against the windowpane. Just before the sun dropped under the horizon and the alley went dark, I noticed something new. There was an arm's-length space between the round woman and the woman with the extraordinary hands. They seemed to be leaving a gap between them wide enough for another man, or a fifth woman, to stand in.

I stared into the gap until my eyes tired in the dark. She never came. I got into bed, and, without warning, they stopped talking. Maybe they had run out of things to say. There was a beat of silence, the first that day. And then the five of them began to hum, in tune, in harmony, the man's voice higher than the women's.

A PAIR OF SUNFISH

There were days in my new apartment, during the first months after my lover Michelle died, when time was elastic. I would wake up in the middle of the night and think it was morning, or I would wake up in the morning and the room would be dark.

Once, I woke at midnight and what appeared to be the afternoon sun already lay across the room. The building and streets and alley were quiet. I got out of bed and walked across the bedroom into the living room. The light was a swath of yellow fabric unfurled across the writing table, gray carpet, and small sofa. I walked in and out of the warmth, the heat rolling over me. My hand in the light glowed and reminded me of a sunfish.

I stood there swimming my hand through the light, then both hands, a pair of sunfish in the sun lake.

There was a line in my palm I had never noticed before. A deep wrinkle that started at my wrist and went straight up to the padding at the bottom of my middle finger; it cut through the life line and the heart line. I looked at the other palm: the line was there, but instead of going straight up to the middle finger, the new line on this palm curved toward my pinky. I sat on the floor, my upper body and head in the light and my legs outside the light, and contemplated this arrival. Was I dreaming? I didn't know.

I went about my night as if it were afternoon. I sat at my writing table and wrote on my thesis, describing how the use of place in x differed from the use of place in y. I talked about how place and time could not be split one from the other, time being an inextricable element of place and place of time. For humans, I concluded in an overly long sentence, time was the lung or skin of place. Though as soon as I wrote that down I thought, no, time was more like oxygen and place breathes it. I was beginning to get lost in my own ideas, which kept shifting as I looked back on them or forward into the blank space on the page at the tip of my pen. Did time precede place or did time need a place to spread into before it could exist?

When I was finished writing about place, I got up and went into the kitchen, and even though the kitchen clock told me it was three o'clock in the morning, the light in the room said early evening. I began making supper. I opened a bag of split peas and added water to a pot. I washed and cut a zucchini, a red onion, a carrot, and a potato. The apartment building was quiet, and I could feel the other inhabitants sleeping; I could feel the sleepiness of the building and the sleepiness of the streets and the City, though I was wide awake and ready to eat supper.

When the peas were cooked I added the vegetables. I ate the soup at my writing table, which was now a dinner table. The light faded, and evening began to sit in the room with me. I read my book on the sofa and listened and watched the day turn into night; the yellow swath of sun vanished and the room filled with dusk. I turned on a lamp and read some more.

My mind began to wander, as it did at night, over the room, the building, and the City. Over the geography of my life. My mind was a field mouse roaming the countryside, sniffing here and there, resting at hilltops and looking out over the vista of trees, rivers, and lakes. This roaming was a lot about texture and impression, though I could sometimes make out a face or hear a snippet of conversation from the past. I heard someone say, *This is how you know when it's ripe,* and another person said, *Welcome to the area.*

I saw Michelle's face, as I often did while I lived in that apartment above the alley, and still do on occasion, when I'm home sick, or when I'm brushing my teeth in front of the hall-way mirror or looking out the wide kitchen window into the green of my backyard. But that night something different happened. Her black eyes looked even more beautiful than when she was alive. Her hand reached toward me in the now dark room, and I took it.

After a while, I don't know how long, the sounds of morning rose up in the hallways. Doors opening and closing, keys in locks, footsteps.

But I sat on the sofa in my particular darkness and did not move one single muscle. I was a sunfish in the middle of a deep lake, hovering close to the weedy bottom between the reeds and boulders. I did not blink. I did not swallow. I did not breathe.

THE OCEAN

A deviant ray of late-morning sun slammed in through my third-story window and knocked me out. I grabbed a pillow from the bed and lay down in the thick of it. Why not? I had no place to go, no plans, only my thesis, and the thesis would wait, would always wait. I fell into a sleep that was very deep.

The telephone rang. It rang four times but my machine didn't pick it up. "Hello," I said.

The voice dragged out horribly; it sounded like a recording of a monster at half speed. "*Hello*." It was creepy, but I didn't feel scared.

"Who is this?" I asked.

"*This is the cow that jumped over the moon,*" he said, in the same gummy, gooey horror-story voice.

"Marc?" I said. "Is this you? " He had liked to play annoying practical jokes and had an uncanny ability to alter his voice. Once, in high school, he had called me, imitating a police officer, and then he questioned me about selling marijuana until I burst out crying and confessed, even though I had never bought or sold marijuana.

"How'd you guess," he said, and now his voice was back to normal, or as normal as a dead person's voice can be. "Listen," he said, "someone here wants to talk to you." The word *here* seemed strange—where was here? I could hear cars halting and then lurching forward.

I walked over to my window and looked down and sure enough there was Marc. He was wearing the front half of a Holstein costume we wore to eighth-grade Halloween—and holding the Holstein's head. The back end of the cow swished vigorously and widely, and a long black-and-white tail swung from left to right as if to hail me. I opened the window and stuck out my head.

"Who is that in the hind end?" Just then the tail lifted up and the sound of loud flatulence filled the air, and then laughing. Marc opened his mouth and bellowed from the gut: "Mmmmmwooooooh." *That's my boy,* I thought, *pitch perfect.* Suddenly the hind end deflated and a red curly head popped out of the cow's back section.

"Julia," I called down. She looked spectacular, radiant, even better than in high school, her bountiful hair blazing and her skin glowing, if a little pale.

They stood there on the street in their limp, now-shapeless cow suit grinning up at me with their unusually white and even teeth. One of the benefits of death, I thought.

"How long has it been since you've been to the ocean?" she yelled up.

I started to explain that in my free time I had to write my thesis but she cut me off.

"That's what I thought. All that ocean and no time to see it. Well, now's the time," she said, dropping out of her cow suit altogether and kicking it into the street.

"Yeah," Marc said, dropping the head on the sidewalk. "Now's the time."

The dead do not easily take no for an answer. They got me to put on my overcoat and cap and we jumped an N-Judah train five blocks away. On the train I barraged them with questions about the afterlife. But they just looked at each other and laughed. "Oh, please," Julia said, dismissively. "Life has made you so boring."

Where the hell have I been? I thought, when I stood before the ocean. It was black and hellish and beautiful. You could see whitecaps far, far out, frothy white foam in the absolute darkness like souls riding the waves, and it reminded me of everything vast and holy and irreproachable. I felt the smallness of my life, but also, maybe, the unnecessary narrowness. My heart broke out of my chest and cantered for the water.

Julia shed her clothes and loped across the beach into

the waves. Her long white limbs and back lit the darkness, a shadowy line up the center of her back as if her body were split by a bottomless ravine. On the train I had checked the windows to see if my dead visitors made a reflection and they didn't. Otherwise they seemed extraordinarily, vibrantly alive, more alive than when they had been alive in high school and leaning in corners at parties sucking on cigarettes and dope until the future was lofted away by clouds.

"Come in!" she shouted, waving at me, and then she dove into a foamy crest and disappeared. A moment later, the water lifted her up, her halo of red hair an offering to the cerulean sky.

I shed my tennis shoes and socks. "Are you going in?" I asked Marc.

"Shhhh," he said. "I'm communing." Deadness had not made him less irritating.

He had laid himself flat out at the sandy edge and flapped his arms and legs. He was making a beach angel. An image popped up in my mind of the glistening snow angels we would make all afternoon in our front yards. He looked up at me intently. "Why do you look so old?" he asked.

"I'm only twenty-seven," I said.

"Then join me," he said. "We can make an army." He smiled with his beautiful teeth, flapping himself deeper and deeper into the sand.

But I had my ocean heart to consider. I dropped my watchman's cap on the sand, tore off my jeans and my shirt and raced toward the impossibly and nearly perfect water.

The cold seized me. It was like a metal cinch up my spine and my muscles threw a fit and my blood plunged toward my rib cage to flee the assault. It felt great! It felt like the best sex I'd ever had! I dove under a wave and my skull exploded in confusion—behind my lids splashed patches of orange and red. Oh, and my lungs! My lungs hardly knew what to do; they gusted like overfilled sails, slamming erratically against my ribcage. Even my lips and fingernails were ecstatic—I could feel them having tiny conniptions and I could feel my earlobes and eyelashes and the tiny bones in my ears (stirrup, anvil, and Santa Maria) chatter and sing. I threw myself over a wave and shouted, "Hallelujah!" And then I shouted it again and I meant it.

I swam through wave after wave, the salt brining my eyes and skin. Julia breezed through the water, slipping under and gliding back up like a seal. She broke through the breakers into the serene flatness. I had never seen anyone swim that far out on Ocean Beach.

"Julia," I called out.

I had read an article about sharks descending on Ocean Beach, traveling solo from the island coasts of Alaska, hungry. A month earlier, one of them had eaten the leg of a surfer.

"Julia," I called out again. "Sharks!" But of course she couldn't hear me, and she wouldn't have listened if she could, she never did. Apparently, death also didn't bring common sense, or any kind of sense I could understand.

Just as I thought this, a familiar-looking gray dorsal fin broke into the story. The shark was lighter gray than the black water and glided evenly and mechanically toward Julia.

I yelled again. "Shark! Really I am not kidding!"

The shark propelled itself toward Julia's legs as she swam like food obliviously toward the horizon. It was like the opening scene in *Jaws*, which Julia, Marc, and I had seen together our senior year at the Saint Cloud theatre. Afterward we ran screaming through the J. C. Penney parking lot, because it really felt to us almost every day that year like we were about to be eaten, and indeed, Julia, who had promised me she'd stay with Marc, had driven home alone that night, after downing a few more beers in the front seat of her father's car, and exploded into the telephone pole.

But in this scene Julia sailed safely forward, her hair brighter and brighter and at the same time shrinking until I saw only a red dot. And then nothing but the horizon's backlit peach and yellow ribbons.

Mark lay asleep inside an angel. Popped out from the sand were his face and knees and toes.

"Julia is wafting out to sea," I said, morosely. I sat down next to him.

He opened one eye. "Think about it," he said, and he dropped his chin and gave me a familiar condescending look, the one he brought back with him from London and New York his first year out of college—it was the last look he'd given me from his hospital bed, and then he rolled out of our cold Midwestern city on Kaposi's brain lesions and morphine.

The sun was abandoning us.

The air on my salty skin stung. My lungs burned.

Despite his wishes to be cremated and fed to the lions at Como Park Zoo, or shot out of a cannon, or dropped onto the Eiffel Tower, or fed to his Abyssinian cat, the family buried him in the town cemetery with his aunts and uncles, toward the back near the fire road and the raspberry bushes.

Hours later I stood up and looked out over the shore. The beach bloomed with hundreds of angels.

THE PARTY

As we walked I stared too long into the westbound wind and my eyes started to ache.

"Are you crying?" Michelle asked.

"No, it's just the wind," I said.

She curved her head and torso around to see my face under my wide-brimmed sunhat, which I had taken to wearing even in the fog, and through my tears I saw her face. But it was distorted; one eye seemed to merge with the other and her nose flattened. And then she disappeared, and we were walking parallel again.

I liked these visual distortions. I liked how they gave me a reprieve from reality. They didn't happen often enough.

We returned to walking in silence. We were not getting along.

We had been getting along well for months, biking through the City and painting the living room and rereading aloud *Wuthering Heights*. And then suddenly we seemed to hate each other, or, if not hate, some sort of primal dislike. That morning we had bickered like magpies over the last bowl of Cheerios.

"You had the last bowl last time," Michelle said.

"You disgust me," I said. She stood back as if I'd punched into her windpipe. I walked into our bedroom with the box and shut the door and then sat on the bed and ate the cereal dry out of the box, feeling this stiff, almost unbearable new shame drop into my stomach. And yet, for some reason that I was unable to articulate or narrate to myself, I couldn't say, "I'm sorry," which is all it would have taken with Michelle to turn things around. She would have put her hand on my shoulder or my butt and in her charming cattle-rustler way, said, "Well, little missy." And as if her words were meat tenderizer, my heart would soften.

But instead I sat on the bed eating my shame. In the kitchen I heard the mixing bowl clack against the sink. The garbage can lid bit down on the plastic liner. A drawer whinnied open and then banged shut.

How did we get into these places? Neither of us had been in a serious relationship before; we had just moved to the City from our childhood homes in the Midwest. The mood descended like a blinding dust storm. At first we wouldn't notice that we were being cranky, but then one of us would notice, and we wouldn't know what to do. And that morning, it felt to me as if we had always been this way and would always be this way. Michelle might have been more hopeful.

"We're in the other dimension," Michelle said now, as we walked, but I just said, "Mmmhmm," and kept on walking. Despite my gloom, I wasn't ready to step out of that timeline. There must have been something about that place and who I was inside it that I liked. I felt the weight of my body on the ground, very solid, and the sky above me vast and open. My lace-up boots made an unusually confident and sturdy sound against the sidewalk. Here I am in my life, they said. I can do what I want. I don't need you, I don't need anyone.

If I shut my eyes now to picture that moment, I see a boundless ochre pasture lit by a perfect golden sun, me in a prairie bonnet and gingham dress tromping toward the horizon.

We were delivering a pie to a friend. He was really only Michelle's friend, though I had met him once on one of her work sites; they remodeled houses together. It was his thirtieth birthday, and at that time in our lives, our midtwenties, thirty seemed not old exactly, but very adult. Thirty seemed the center of the universe, and our invitation to his party, our first since we moved to the City, made us feel closer to that center. We also felt sure—the thought never even had to formulate—that our status as a couple secured our relevance.

Michelle was carrying the pie. She was carrying the pie balanced on her palms, as if she were presenting an offering to the sun, the air, the grass. She had baked the pie using raspberries from the farmers' market—Eric had requested red. Eric was an artist and designed costumes for fringe theatre from the materials he scavenged from thrift stores. I had made the crust out of whole-wheat pastry flour, and, following my mother's recipe, a teaspoon of vinegar. Michelle was in charge of baking it. "Oh, shit," she said upon opening the oven door. The crust was burned on the edges, little blackened fluted ridges. I stared at the pie and said nothing, though I might have smiled, because I was the one who usually burned things.

"Let's just go," she said. "Before I like you even less than I do now."

"OK," I said, and grabbed my leather jacket and then decided I needed only a sweater. I stomped down the stairs and out the door.

I must admit, despite my mood and the feeling of estrangement between us, or maybe because of it, I could see that Michelle was beautiful. Not in any easy or ordinary way, and probably not the kind of beauty you are imagining now. The geography of her face, the large dark eyes, the nose that started high and then sloped. Her confident cheekbones and fattened-calf lips. "Still, you are beautiful," I said.

She would have none of it. She just shifted the pie to one palm, balancing it like a skillful waiter.

"Do you think I'm beautiful?" I asked. "I mean, from an anthropological perspective."

Michelle had a way of stopping that I admired. She would

be moving, and then she would be stopped, as if she had never been moving. And when she was moving, it seemed she always had been. Whatever she was doing took on the quality of the eternal. And so I wasn't surprised when she turned and stared at me. I looked at the tree over her shoulder, lifting my chin to give her a view of my face unobstructed by eye contact and whatever that thing was that shone through the eyes. I didn't want to bias her with my soul.

"Yes," she said finally. "You are beautiful."

It was the first thing we had agreed upon for a week. But we resumed our walking and the feeling of strangeness remained.

Someone in an oversized Elmo outfit answered the door. "Happy birthday to me!" Eric said. He stood in the doorframe, red and furry from head to toe. His eyes shone through uneven slits. The fabric sagged around his hips and ankles—he looked like a furry red worm. Deflated. Elmo deflated, except for his happy eyes, which created an even more random landscape. A gust of exhaustion hit me; in our early days in the City I often didn't feel up to being interesting. I wanted to go home, but Michelle smiled and did something I had never seen her do before. She dropped to one knee and held out the pie, as if offering a gift to a god. I took a step back and stared at her. Eric leaned forward from the waist, coquettishly, and smelled the pie. But the face had no nose and it made for an odd little scene.

Michelle's theatrical moments usually delighted me—as if inside Michelle lived other Michelles. They popped up the way deer pop up in forests or the way fluorescent moss pokes out of decaying logs. But in that moment I also felt envy; it was as if she and Eric had rehearsed this, as if they had a secret bond that Michelle and I did not have, nor did I have with anyone in the City. I had only Michelle. I could see Elmo's whole body now sparked with happiness.

"What was that?" I mumbled to Michelle as we followed him down the hall. She didn't answer, which was the right thing to do, given my bitter tone and the fact that we were at a party.

About ten people lounged in Eric's living room, all costumed as *Sesame Street* characters. Michelle laughed and waved at them, which made me think she knew them, but she couldn't have, could she? She put her arm around my shoulders, which she hadn't done for a week. "This is the love of my life," she said. "Hello, love of my life," they all yelled back, and, for a moment, I tipped into the familiar weight of Michelle's arm, warm and protective. She had a genuine desire to shelter me and I had a genuine desire to be sheltered. But part of me resisted, the arm began to feel too heavy. I stepped out from under it and stood in front of the wide living room window, the western sky and sun breaking through the fog at my back, heating up my hair.

On the couch, Kermit the Frog snuggled against some character with googly eyes and a mushroom-shaped head. Michelle crossed the room and hugged the mushroom-headed one.

"Cookie Monster," she said. He waddled his head around and Michelle imitated him.

When she was finished saying her hellos she returned to my side by the window, but she crossed her arms over her chest.

"He doesn't have a mouth," I said discreetly.

"Sure he does," she said, without looking at me. "You're the only one who can't see it."

Why was I so hurt and shamed by this remark? Was it her tone? My shoulders constricted. I felt as if a pigeon had been loosed in my face. By the time I could see again, Michelle had disappeared.

A few years ago, I read an article that claimed we experience only six primal emotions: happiness, anger, fear, sadness, disgust, and surprise. Fear is characterized by trembling and tightening of the muscles. Sadness tightens the throat and relaxes the limbs. Surprise, gaping eyes and a dropped jaw, lasts only a moment and is always followed by something else, happiness, anger, fear, or sadness.

All other emotions we develop as adults and are hybrids of these six. Depression and grief a variety of sadness. Pleasure a variety of happiness, and horror a variety of fear. According to psychologist Robert Plutchik, we combine varying degrees of primal emotions to form secondary emotions. Surprise and sadness, for example, produce disappointment, while disgust and anger produce contempt. Anger, fear, and love produce jealousy.

Love was not mentioned in any other part of the article, except to list it amidst a group of thirty secondary emotions. Love socked between hysteria, loneliness, paranoia, and pity.

So what was that feeling, when I looked at Michelle careening like a twelve-year-old boy down our street on her bicycle, or when we lay together on our living room couch, my heart fat and fluttering into all the empty places, lighting up my skin, cocooning me in sunlight? Sometimes, I had to throw my arms around her and squeeze as hard as I could just to contain those feelings.

A month before the party, Michelle and I hiked north of the City under a canopy of redwoods. "Look at that," she said. I pressed up against her from behind, perched my chin on her shoulder, and aligned my gaze. The bird, the burl, the wand of light painted across a furred trunk. "Ahh," I said, though I doubted we were seeing the same thing. "Yes," I said. "Thank you for showing me that." What was the emotion, in those moments, that made the world seem larger yet less chaotic? My blood pressure calmed, my limbs relaxed, my tongue dropped to the floor of my mouth. Did those feelings have anything to do with Michelle?

The article also said that emotions live in the body for only about ninety seconds. If you count to ninety, the emotion, the original emotion, has been blown across the fields. Watch a baby or toddler cry full throated and then suddenly laugh. Sadness, then happiness, then sadness again.

Bert and Ernie lounged on the floor on either side of the coffee table. "I'm hot," one of them said. "God, I'm suffocating in here," the other said.

Two other characters, one pink and one purple, were aiming glasses of beer at their small mouth holes; one of them had to pull the fabric up to align the hole with its mouth and the other needed to pull the fabric down. "Here, let me help." They poured beer into each other's mouths, laughing.

Eric had sewn each outfit but had neglected certain details. Everyone had beautifully crafted ears—even characters I'm not sure were supposed to have ears—but, as I mentioned, eyes and mouths were askew, and some characters, like Cookie Monster, were altogether missing vital parts.

"Will you please scratch my midback?" the pink character said to the brown character, perhaps a dog, that sat behind it. "With what?" the dog said, and wagged his shoulders. The dog had no front legs, but it lay back and shuffled its rear paws against the pink one's back. Big Bird padded out of the kitchen wearing an empty holster.

"Big Bird!" somebody yelled, and then they all shouted as a chorus, and those who had hands clapped and those who didn't, like the dog, just kicked up their legs.

Big Bird sauntered over to my side in front of the window and looked down at me, dark brown eyes staring out from yellow cloth feathers.

"You could be somebody," she said, and bumped me with her feathery elbow. She was wearing yellow cleaning gloves.

"I am somebody," I said.

"Eric made Oscar the Grouch."

I knew Big Bird meant this as a humorous bridge—I knew

that. I could have laughed. And yet the rolling blank fields of silence made a pleasant whistle deep in my ears.

More recently, I read an article that said the puppeteer of Elmo was accused of molesting minors. I remember feeling sad, but also something else—a kind of confirmation of my own morbid distrust of funny voices and primary hues? I also read that if you put a child under the age of two in front of a television program, the child's brain revs into hyperdrive. You begin to destroy the child's ability to discern nuanced emotions and moods. When I read these articles, the first thing I wanted to do was call Michelle. But of course, Michelle was long gone.

At the party, Big Bird shook her large cone-shaped head and waddled away with big floppy orange feet.

A trail of sunlight slanted in through the window behind me and touched the coffee table, which I noticed was clear glass, and painted a leaf shape on the green rug.

"You're looking at something," someone said. On the floor to my right the only person sitting solo was looking up at me. She wore a pink mask and a black cowboy hat.

"Which *Sesame* character are you?" I asked.

"I'm just a cowboy," she said. She yodeled several times, guileless and mournful; it echoed into the room and took shape, like the leaf, near the ceiling.

"You are a star," I said. And I meant it. It was the first moment that week that I felt truly generous.

"Thank you," the cowboy said. We continued looking at each

other for a while, and then something else happened and we looked away.

Sometimes, on Sunday nights, Michelle and I huddled around our small television on our orange shag living room rug, watching *Bonanza* reruns, our technological campfire burning romantic images of the western frontier into our brains. The feeling in that living room—a certain kind of refuge, while I imagined heading out on my own horse across the dusty plains.

In one episode, Little Joe was bitten by a snake, and before the toxins pulsed into his heart, he had to sever his own hand. The family had left him alone on the ranch. Scene by scene the hand bloated like a fresh snake's corpse, the gray skin distending and thinning over his knuckles. Just as he was pressing the butcher knife to his wrist, someone galloped up and stopped him. But in my mind he cut the hand off, and I deeply admired him for it.

"Do you think you could do that?" I asked Michelle when we shut down the screen.

"I think I could," she answered. "If I absolutely had to."

That night the winds blew through the walls of our apartment. I stared at my wrist in the dark, how the veins, arteries, and bone fed into the white flesh of my palm.

I had lost track of Big Bird, until she walked out of the hallway back through the living room and into the kitchen, her tail feathers clumped on one side. A few minutes later the kitchen door swung open and Big Bird sauntered out holding up the pie alight with candles. Cookie Monster followed with a carton of ice cream. They stood with Elmo in front of the glass coffee table.

There must have been thirty candles, for Eric's thirty years, crowded on the pie. The whole top was aflame—a gold disk of light floated above the crust.

"Happy birthday to you," we all sang as Michelle presented the pie with her yellow-gloved hands to Elmo, who jumped back and forth, and then everybody got up, even Bert and Ernie from the floor, and jumped up and down. Big Bird looked at me and I looked back. I thought about Eric, who was spinning and jumping and singing "Happy Birthday to me," and I gave a little hop.

But that disk of flame over the pie had captivated me. I wish someone had taken a photo but they were busy jumping and singing. I stared at the flame. Like a light parfait, at the base of the orange and yellow glowed a thin blue.

Then something floated down, a yellow feather from Big Bird, and I heard a loud popping sound. There was an orange flash of fire, and then the pie flew out of Big Bird's rubber gloves and landed on Eric, who stopped spinning as the fire clutched his synthetic red fur and gobbled Elmo's torso until it was half aflame.

Something in the universe shifted then, and in blew one of those distortions. I saw the flame crawl from Elmo, to Cookie Monster, to Bert, as if it were determined to burn all that happiness. One by one each furry costume caught and blossomed into an orange cone of flame. Big Bird was the last to go, her feathers snapping and popping.

And then the universe shifted again and only Eric was screaming.

Thank god, everyone said. Thank god I had not donned a costume myself and could use my arms and legs. Everyone had just stood there in mid cheer, helpless, or else they would have gone up too. If the woolen blanket hadn't been on the chair next to me, if I had been sitting on it and not noticed it.

Thank god, thank god, thank god.

Later, we all sat on the floor and talked and stared at each other. Eric, bare-chested and unscathed, only a little pink, sat next to me in the middle of the room, people circled around us. Big Bird was Michelle again. Bert and Ernie and all their cohorts had human faces.

What is this life? we all asked.

The people at the party didn't become my friends, but I saw them at other parties and they always remembered me, even after we stopped talking about the fire. And many of the details had blurred. But, for me, those first few minutes after I threw the blanket over him have stayed bright. We were standing around with our mouths agape. Michelle stood about five feet away from me. We were looking directly at each other, my face still sweaty and hot. But Michelle did not come toward me, she didn't touch me. She was looking at me with an expression—awe and mistrust and something else. What is inside that space between us? I could see she was frightened, and I also felt frightened. What is it about love that makes us so mortal? I suddenly felt an immense, vast isolation—as if I had stepped off the edge of an endless gorge into the dark and cold.

Two years later, I stood in the chilled air of a city morgue, and a woman in a white lab coat pulled back a bright white sheet. I thought I would feel horror or revulsion, that something inside me would crack. But none of that happened.

"Stand on this side," the woman said, and gently guided me around.

Michelle's eyes were closed—probably the woman or the paramedics had closed them. She looked just like Michelle only paler. Even though I knew the back of her skull had fractured in the bike accident and that she was dead, I expected her breath to be warm, and for her to make her soft whistly breathing sounds that I listened to in the middle of the night, sometimes early morning, when I lay awake dreaming into the sound of my future.

"I feel sick," I said at the party. I dropped to my knees and hung my head between my legs. I could still taste the Cheerios in the back of my throat. An almost unbearable pressure expanded inside my ribcage. People were staring at me and I began to sob. I held on to the coffee table, littered with ash and singed red fur and bits of piecrust.

"You were amazing," Eric said, and he put his arms around me and laid his cheek against mine. "You saved me!"

On the walk home, Michelle took my hand, and I held on tight.

"Would you ever have thought I could do something like that?" I asked. To my surprise, Michelle nodded. "Yes."

A MAN OLDER THAN ME,
BUT STILL YOUNG

Sometimes, I sat at my small table by the window and imagined a man older than me, but still young, sitting with me, his long fingers holding my best teacup. The alley below empty, the windows in the building across the alley empty, the plant on the table blooming its purple flowers in the morning light and then the afternoon light and then the evening light. In my mind he steadily returned my gaze. I had not felt that kind of love since childhood, certainly not since I lived in that apartment, but during that time, the man really did help me. I told him about the sounds of grief in the alley, the malleability of time, shifting shadows and light, isolation, dreams, the sewage system, broken things, colors, closets, phone calls, stains making shapes on carpet, my red pants, ants and squirrels, the materialization of cornbread, the gaps between people, the company of furniture. I would say, *The lover becomes memory and memory becomes an artifact, a sacred tomb.*

I offered him more tea.

It's nice to have someone to listen to, he said, gazing steadily back at me, something in his expression more ample than realism. He told me the good news, our hearts cradled in sacrificial light, shepherds braying with sheep, bread and fish, buoyancy of water, two palms open to us, vast skies, pearly gates, corpses rising, birds in flight, the feeling of acceptance for all beings, this feeling sometimes so insistent he felt he would explode.

Sometimes we didn't even talk. Sometimes I think those times were the best.

And now, so many years later, as I sit at my computer in my office, I think how soothing that would be to have Jesus here again. What is the harm, really? To be accompanied by his enormous goodwill and kindness, even for a little while. Even if it isn't real.

The lover lives in us, he said. *In the seas, in the fur of horses and dogs and bears, in the fins of fish, in grass and seeds, lamplight and sun-light and lungs and sidewalks.*

THE LETTER

On the roof of the apartment building, in the middle of a hot day a few months before I moved out, I found a letter from a woman named Norse to a woman named Solange. The envelope was sealed, worn and soiled with the tread marks of shoes. It had never been mailed. The letter also had been rained on, perhaps numerous times over two or three rainy seasons. Norse's address had vanished, but the address of Solange was legible.

It was the kind of hot day that takes you by surprise and unsettles you. By noon the heat drove me into the hallway of the building, but I didn't want to go outside onto the streets. I walked toward the stairs and looked up. I had always imagined the door to the roof was locked, but when I turned the handle it opened.

The letter was handwritten. Most of the lines had been washed away but I could see the following:

Dear Solange,
We have been invaded by silences

A few lines below that I found, stuck to the page, a long black eyelash.

And just below that:

. the house with dark windows and dark gates.

I sat on the roof and read those lines again and again. The sidewalks and concrete buildings below me shimmered and sparkled—someone had told me they mixed ground quartz in the concrete.

Dear Solange, I thought.

I am up on the roof reading your letter. It is a hot day. I don't do well with heat, but I am drinking a lot of water and perhaps will buy a fan. I wonder what weather you are having.

And then a few minutes later, I thought this. *Dear Solange, What does it mean—the house with dark windows and dark gates? Were you to meet someone there? And is the silence between you and Norse?*

I took the letter downstairs into my apartment. The next day I read it again and I wrote.

Dear Solange,
Sometimes behind my closed eyelids I see a yellow circle.

And the next day.

Dear Solange,

I am closing my eyes now—white halos and a square of orange.

I kept the letter in my bedroom on my chest of drawers. The hot days cooled and filled with winds that blew me around the City like a sailboat, blew me down Market Street to work and blew me home, and for the first time I noticed that the iron grates on the windows made music as they chinked against their loose hinges.

Dear Solange,

The apartment is singing.

Dear Solange,

Last night I saw a house with dark windows and gates. I knocked on the door but no one answered.

The next day I wrote.

Dear Solange,

I want to watch television, the one I don't own yet, something funny.

I started carrying the letter around with me in my coat pocket when I wore a coat, as I did the next week when the cold rains began. Sometimes, when it wasn't raining, I carried the letter in my jeans pocket.

Dear Solange,

I saw a raccoon in the street yesterday. Its black mask matched the tar.

I thought about mailing Norse's letter. There was a stamp, but of course it wasn't enough now and it was stained and peeling off at the edges. I went to the post office and bought stamps; the clerk was kind and helpful.

Dear Solange,

I have lived alone in this apartment for two years, but I am beginning to believe I will not always be alone. I am beginning to see people again, and speak to them.

I thought about mailing the letter every time I walked down Market Street to work and passed a mailbox and when I walked home. I thought about mailing the letter inside another envelope and with a real note of my own. My real note would say:

> Dear Solange,
>
> I found this letter on the roof of my apartment building. I thought you might want to have it. I am moving soon to a new apartment and I don't need it anymore.

The rains ended and the ficus tree outside my building perked up its leaves. A week before I moved out, I wrote the note and put it in a clean envelope with Norse's letter, and readdressed the envelope, using no return address.

It was a foggy morning, but I knew, we all knew, that the fog would burn off in an hour and the still sun would warm our faces. A woman walking on the street in front of me wore a long red sweater and red boots. She had sleek black hair and a willowy gait. I walked behind her for several blocks. I stood behind her at the stoplights, matched my pace to hers, six paces back. In the middle of a block, she suddenly turned in a slow full circle and looked directly at me. She had pale skin and gray eyes. The fog more like mist. She was smiling. I cocked my head and smiled back.

A slow full circle, and then she turned down Sansome Street.

THE CRACK

The City cranes demolished the apartment building on the alley less than one month after I received my final notice to move out, the brick and mortar and plaster caving in easily, explosions of white and red dust pluming up into a blue sky.

For the two years I lived on the third floor, a crack in the ceiling that started above the door stretched the short length of the living room. The crack had been plastered over many times before I moved in, the paint and plaster buckling and flaking off onto my sofa in small geological shapes. If I leaned back and rested my head on the sofa's back, I could glare at the crack, which sometimes resembled a river and other times a canyon or a ravine.

The building was already falling apart. In the night, I listened to the walls erupt in bumps and thumps and creaking sounds.

After a few months, I called up the manager.

"I'm wondering about that crack in the ceiling," I said.

She seemed to be expecting me. "Enjoy that," she said, with a French Caribbean accent. "That won't hurt you." I thought she was joking, but her tone was sincere.

A week later, on a Sunday afternoon, I heard her laughing in the hallway, loud and fluid. I had been lying on the couch, but I got up and stepped outside to reintroduce myself and ask again about the crack. "Ah, you are that one," she said, and laughed some more. It made her round face and hair look like the moon or a Happy Face. I admit I thought of the manager more as a symbol, the Keeper of Keys or the Icon of Infrastructure, than a real person. But I also didn't feel much like a real person myself. I didn't speak to anyone in the building. I just went to my job as a receptionist at CrackerBrokers Inc., where the phones never rang, and came home to my apartment. I should have been somebody's hamster instead of a person.

But I was curious about the manager. She wore bright solid colors: that day in the hallway she wore purple pants and a purple shirt and purplish lipstick. The next time I saw her, when my toilet broke, she arrived (a week later) as the color pink. Even her shoes were pink, and though I was angry about her reluctant response to the toilet and the crack, for the outfits I admired her and was grateful. I imagined she awakened every morning feeling like a certain color, and then she took that feeling all the way—she drove straight at the sentiment.

Years before I moved into that building, I had met a middle-aged woman in a women's studies class who was similarly committed to color. Every class she wore a different vibrant pair of colors: one week she'd show up in pink pants and a blue shirt, the next she'd be wearing yellow and green. Though I can't remember her name, she gave, in our final class, a heartbreaking report on the Soviet Gulag system. At its peak, the Gulag consisted of over four hundred official prisons holding millions of inmates, including political prisoners, Jews, dissidents. In the 1950s, she had spent three years in the Gulag, sitting in a concrete room with ten other women. During the day they dug holes for fence posts and sewed the guards' uniforms. She said she wore the same top and pants the entire three years, the same gray color as the walls, never washed so the fabric grew stiff and scratchy.

At that time in my life, and for many years after, I didn't understand the liberating power of pigment, hue, and saturation.

After the toilet broke the heater died. The temperature dropped to near freezing. That was the year it snowed in the City and everyone stayed inside. In the night I dreamed I was on my knees shivering in the living room and praying to the Virgin Mary, but instead of her face when I looked up I saw the manager looking down at me with something like benevolence. And, like the toilet, she did, eventually, fix the heater.

Every day I went to my job and came home and glared at

the crack. It was the same day after day. But then one evening, toward the end of my stay in the building, I leaned back and saw it had begun to grow. Instead of stopping outside my bedroom, which was really an adjunct to the living room, the line had pushed inside and was wider. The dark center had thickened. By Saturday, when I woke at noon, the crack was nearly over my bed.

I called the manager.

"The crack is growing," I said.

"Going?" she laughed. "Going where?"

I didn't laugh. "It's over my bed."

"What are you doing still in your bed?" she asked.

She said she would visit in an hour.

I got up and dressed in my burgundy jeans and red shirt, which I hadn't worn since I moved into the building. It was a holiday weekend, and I hadn't been outside for days. It was very blue out the window—a very dark blue sky and a very dark blue light. I went out into that light to buy bread and milk and a can of tuna. Despite my fears and anger about the crack, I thought maybe the manager would be hungry and we could eat something together.

But as I walked, I felt more and more annoyed. Really, she should have fixed the crack long ago, I thought. What if my ceiling collapses on me? What if no one hears it? Who would know and who would find me? But then I thought, *It really isn't her fault*, because she doesn't own the building and probably has no control over restoration and repair. I also felt bad for the manager on a personal level, imagining her living alone with pet reptiles, nothing but the suffering of some past in Haiti now transformed into this resolute happiness, much like the woman who had suffered in the Gulag.

As I opened the can of tuna and made sandwiches, waiting for the manager to arrive, I wondered what color she woke to that day. Orange would be good, or perhaps yellow.

She showed up finally in late afternoon, after I had eaten both sandwiches, dressed in an amber pantsuit with large amber earrings and copper lips. Despite my unhappiness, I had to admit the ensemble was lovely with the blue skies of the day. Nonetheless I decided to take a stand.

"I want the crack fixed immediately," I said. "It's hazardous."

"Hazardous?" she said.

"Yes, I won't live like this any longer, it's inhuman."

"In yuman," she agreed, staring at my face from her amber face with the same benevolent expression she had in my dream. Just then, a piece of plaster shaped like an evergreen tree landed on my red shirt.

"See," I said, pointing to my chest. "How can you expect me to go on living like this?"

But instead of answering, she walked toward my bed and stood and stared at the crack and its dark center, her neck stretched so far back I could see the ridges of her veins and muscles. She stood looking for a long time, and I stood next to her. Suddenly, the dark center of the crack began to widen, and then the ceiling split open like a skin, and we could see the apartment upstairs. Without moving her head, the manager reached over and backhanded me, on my upper arm. It was the first passionate human contact I had had since I moved into the building. "Look at that," she said, and she smiled like she knew this was going to happen. Soon the notices to move would start arriving in the mail, but I didn't know that then. Her arm was by her side again and she was still looking up. "Just wait," she said. We waited a full minute. Then the upstairs ceiling opened, and the blue sky and golden light of the day poured in.

THE RAVINE

A-hunting we will go, a-hunting we will go,
Heigh-ho, the derry-o, a-hunting we will go.

I woke up at six o'clock on Saturday and decided I would hunt. I pulled on my jeans, T-shirt and old brown shoes. My father had worn thick leather boots. I folded my hair under my red hunting hat and stuffed some peanuts and an apple into my coat pocket. The 56 bus took me over the Golden Gate Bridge, and when I saw some woods I got out.

The woods were immediately dark and quiet, though I could hear the faint whistle of traffic behind me. The darkness and quiet said, *Here we are, here we are, together again. What have you been doing with your time?*

I felt accused. *I sit in my apartment and write my thesis,* I said. In my mind, I began trotting out the details that make a daily life, and then the larger accomplishments that accumulate over the years, and the things I had yet to do or planned someday to finish, but no matter how I added it up, my life looked small and unimpressive, though not without its excuses. *Indeed,* I thought. *What have I been doing with my time?*

I walked on, over the dried leaves and branches, and then over pine needles, deeper into the silence of the woods. My hunting hat made my scalp sweat and itch: I took it off and tucked it into my jeans; I was glad no one was there to witness the dirge of my pale forehead. A song came into my head:

> The worms crawl in
> The worms crawl out
> The worms play pinochle in my snout

I hummed the children's song over and over, and I walked and walked into the woods. I sat down and adjusted my shoe. A tiny rock had sneaked into the heel of my inner sock, and I had to sit and stare at that phenomenon for a while—I was impressed with its tenacity. I put the pebble in my pocket and took out the baggie of peanuts. I began shelling and eating the peanuts, though I wasn't really hungry and knew it was a bad idea not to wait; later I would have nothing but the apple.

A bird flew down through the tree line, and then flew back up out of sight. A few minutes later it dropped onto a lower branch. My thesis was about animals in literature, but it had been a long time since I'd thought about the actual life of a

North American woods animal, or about the insect or bug. A squirrel ran down a tree and sat at the base and watched me. *What have you been doing?* I asked the squirrel.

Today I am staring into the darkness, listening to the wind, cracking things open, scratching my hide. I also am looking for feathers and fur for the inner lining of my drey. What are you doing here?

I'm hunting, I said.

You don't have a gun, the squirrel said.

I put on my hat and swung my rifle in its canvas sack around to the front. The squirrel leapt onto the tree and disappeared. The bird that had been perched on the low branch flew away. Nobody wants to talk about death, about getting caught off guard by a predator like me. I took the rifle out of its sack; it was time to get serious.

I walked another mile into the woods, without seeing any more animals, which made me think the earlier ones had sent out a warning—only fair and good. When I reached a ravine, I stood at the edge and looked into the deep thicket and the darker air, and then I looked into an even denser darkness, balled like yarn, and I waited for my pupils to dilate. There was a clearing through the center of the brush, and I could see, at the bottom, about twenty yards down, a deer. The deer was looking up toward me, a buck with no prongs yet. It was standing on a piece of wood. I lifted my rifle and squared the butt on my shoulder, and then I looked through the scope. The head of the deer flew into my vision. I moved the sight to its white chest and stiffened my shoulder. I steadied my aim and pulled the trigger and stumbled back.

My body had not forgotten the force of the gun, but I had forgotten the smell of gunpowder, acrid and metallic, and the blue haze that lingers for a moment like a pungent spirit.

The deer was gone.

I put the gun back into its canvas sack and slung it behind me. I hiked into the ravine, descending over fallen trees, stumps, brambles, vines and brush, all the things of a ravine. A bramble snagged my little finger and I cursed. The ravine said, *What are you doing here?* I replied, *I'm trying to get to the bottom of all this.*

The ravine was silent, and rightly so. I hiked further down into it. At the bottom I saw that the piece of wood was a door, an old kitchen door, the green paint chipped off entirely except for a patch in the center. There was a black doorknob. It looked like the door that led to a porch in the first apartment I lived in, with Michelle.

One evening while I was at work, she kicked a hole through one of the lower panels. Her boot caught and she couldn't remove it and so she sat on the floor of the porch and waited for me to come home. I remember walking into the living room and seeing her leather boot dangling above the splintered wood; it looked like a trophy. I unlaced and removed the boot and helped her slip her bare foot back through the hole. Michelle's foot—brown and slender with a silver ankle bracelet, the second toe strangely longer than the other toes, and wide at the bulb. The toe was an eye staring at me. The door was staring also.

You probably think I'm going to open it; you think the door is a portal to another world, perhaps where Michelle is still alive.

I sat down on the door and ate the apple, contemplating how objects when taken out of context gather meaning—like the door for example—how did it get there? On the edge of the door was a drop of the deer's blood. I thought about this for a long time as I ate my apple. The wind had crept into the ravine and was whirling with leaves. The quiet and the darkness were waiting for the hunter to make her next move.

Although I would have been content to sit on the door longer, maybe for the rest of my life, my father had taught me what to do. I got up, and I picked my way up the other side of the ravine, which still had nothing to say. The wood's floor was not as thick on this side as it had been on what was now the *other* other side. Half-decayed logs, balled patches of dried dirt. As I climbed, I could see that the ravine was steeper than I had imagined, or rather than my legs forecasted on my descent, and I noted, not for the first time, the relationship between effort and distance. It felt good to climb a ravine on a Saturday morning and to be in the company of the woods, and not in my apartment alone working on my thesis. A brown worm crawled out of a hole in a log. It was tunneling deeply into the soil and mixing subsoil with topsoil, secreting its slime to give the plants nitrogen and to aggregate soil particles.

Do you ever get lonely? I asked.

I have air, the worm said. *I have dirt, I have decay; inside this log where I live there is a dead squirrel. Someday I will have you,* the worm said.

Not yet, I said.

I can wait, the worm said.

I climbed up the ravine into the lighter air at the top, where the trees were thinner and taller, and they laid a sheet of golden leaves at my feet. The sun hummed a little song, several high notes followed by a few lower notes. I walked faster; my rifle in its canvas sack skipped and hopped and jogged against my hip. *Here we are,* I thought, *together again. Is this how you feel?* I asked the sun, trees, air, dirt, and leaves. *Shhhhh. Shhhhh,* they said. And I respected their privacy.

I slowed my walk and tried to pay attention to the wood's floor, looking for deer blood, a disheveled path. I wound my way through trees, which were becoming thicker and denser again, only a dribble of light here and there.

Goodbye, the light said.

Au revoir, I said.

You can always turn back, the light said.

I have to track the wounded deer and shoot it again, better this time, and then drag it from the woods to butcher and freeze, perhaps to give meat to a shelter.

You could leave it for us, said the air, the worms, and the magpie.

Or me, said the bear.

I hadn't thought about bears; perhaps one hid behind some tree or boulder. Maybe the magpie was impersonating a bear so I would turn back.

You smell good, the bear said.

I said, *I thought grizzlies had been driven out of California and most of the United States.* The bear didn't answer or speak again.

I walked on and on into the thicker woods, past a fallen naked tree, a huddle of gray-stemmed red-capped mushrooms, a hut-sized boulder that was covered in lichen, a silence that remained fertile and silent. I saw the deer. It was leaning against the trunk of a tree. I unsheathed my gun again and lowered to one knee to brace the gun. And I shot, and the pungent spirit of the deer appeared, and the deer dropped.

The darkness and the quiet sighed.

The deer lay crumpled on its front legs, muzzle to the ground. I turned the deer over and I pulled out my leather gloves and rope. The leg joints loosened and wrapped behind the head. I fastened the rope around the deer's neck and legs the way my father had shown me, and then I began dragging the deer, a small buck, in its first fall and now never winter, back toward the ravine. I felt a sense of accomplishment and said so to the deer. The deer said, *My eyes eyeless now.*

Resting and breathing deeply in ten-foot intervals, smelling the hide and the stirred-up ground, I dragged the dead body of the deer. The air entered the wound and turned it dank. I pulled and pulled until I hit the ravine and then sat down with my legs over the edge and wondered what to do. I asked a bird, no answer. I asked a squirrel, no answer. I took off my brown jacket and knotted the arms around my waist; the sharp smell of my sweat mingled with that of dead skin. My heart said *pa pa pa*—and my lungs with their oxygen had to catch up. *Yes. Yes. Yes. Go. Go. Go,* my body said. *We forget so easily,* I said. The next day, as I sat at my writing table and read my books, I started the forgetting.

I strapped the deer on a wide log, the way my father had shown me, and then I pushed the log and the deer down into the ravine. The door was still at the bottom. Now I had the feeling that I could open it and reveal, if not an alternate world, at least a tunnel to the other side, maybe all the way to the road where I could catch the bus. But the door was still only a door. Under it was flattened dirt, plants, grass, tree roots, pebbles, and the cracks made by the worms.

How would I get the deer out? *You won't,* said the ravine. *It's just another unfinished project.* I began to feel defensive again, and then I recognized the truth in the statement. I sat down on the door again and wished I had my apple or some peanuts. The deer's legs were stiffening and flies flew back and forth over its cloudy black eyes and its black lips had pulled back from its teeth so I could see its dark purple gums.

You forgot to gut me, the deer said.

I loosed the animal from the log and laid it belly up. From my canvas bag I pulled out my father's butcher knife and hatchet and I slit the deer down the middle. Out of the cavity rose a sheet of steam that said, *Hush, hush,* while blood warmed the ground silently, spattering my shoes. Inside the cavity lay the quiet, rubbery sacs of the heart, lungs, stomach and intestines; I cut and yanked out the entrails. I cut off the deer's legs and split its backbone; I cut off the head; I quartered the torso.

The gutting and quartering took a long time. Part of me was happy *doing* but another part of me was worrying. I worried that the sun would set and leave me lost in the woods, that I would give up and the deer and the hunt would go to waste, that the meat was damaged because I had forgotten to remove the entrails right after shooting it, that I wouldn't have enough time to air the meat properly now and so it would taste gamey; that no one in the City, including me, would want to eat it. I also worried there was something more important I should have been doing with this day, and that perhaps I was often making the wrong decisions about how to spend my days, until my whole adult life was a series of failures and waste.

From the canvas rifle bag I unfurled another canvas bag. The quarters fit like puzzle pieces. I tied the top shut and said good-bye to the deer's head, legs, entrails, and blood. I said goodbye to the worms and the beasts waiting for their own feast.

I put on my coat and hiked up the ravine, dragging the sack of meat in two-foot intervals. I thought several times about leaving the sack behind. I thought a lot about sleeping. I lay down and shut my eyes several times, watching the black background with a string of blue coming in from the left while the flies supped on my blood-soaked arms, and sweat cooled my back, and the quiet and the darkness rushed in to soothe me. I got up. I got up and I dragged the bag of meat behind me over the pine needles and dirt. I went on. The woods grew darker and darker and I inched forward like the worm.

At the edge of the woods I stopped and wiped myself off with leaves and dirt. The traffic whistled.

Goodbye, I said. *Goodbye ravine and door, bird and squirrel and grizzly if you were a grizzly, and worms and vulture and golden leaves and dappled light and foliaged air.*

Goodbye, the darkness and quiet said.

I walked back out of the woods. The air was cool and the earth was turning its back on the light from the day.

I got on the 56 bus, and sat in the back row with my sack of meat on the seat in front of me, and then I moved the sack to the floor for a young man who got on at the next stop. The canvas bag was slowly beginning to turn the floor red. I looked out the window and suddenly my island appeared with its lacy blue edges and green hills, sinking under the weight of the white city.

THE WALK

The sun was taxiing through the clouds and leaving light vapors on the sidewalk. I stepped into light and then shadow and then light again, the air shifting from warm to cool to warm. It was Sunday. I had nowhere to be. I thought about my mother in her house in the cold. The white expanse of her backyard. I could see a crow land in the middle of the yard, and my mother's stroke-stricken face at her window, forehead, nose, and lips pressed against the glass.

At the main street there was a pull to go north, which is the direction I usually walk on that street, and so it took some extra energy to walk south. Even though the road was flat near my house in either direction, I felt as if I were marching uphill. At the small neighborhood park I stopped and lay on my back in the grass. The grass was cool and damp, and my jacket and shirt rode up, so the cool grass pricked my skin. I thought about my mother again. She was walking up the long gravel driveway to fetch the mail. The furred hood of my father's parka hung low over her bowed head, obscuring the top half of her face. She walked with the snow, and flakes collected on the back of the hood and on her shoulders. The driveway was icy and she put her arms out to balance her step, and then she dipped side to side as if she were a hang glider. I was happy to see her being so childlike.

A shadow and cool breeze crept over my face. My eyes were closed but I could feel something panting and staring at me.

Hello, I said.

Hello, the dog said. Do you have anything for me?

I said no, and the dog leapt away.

I got up from the grass and headed south again. Now there were hills, a real hill, and the muscles in my calves and thighs became joyous. Yes! Yes! they shouted. The top of my head was getting closer to the sun. Now, as I walked, I felt my mother walking behind me, in her spring-peach shirt and sun visor. I could hear her practical footsteps and her breathing, which grew heavier as we climbed the green hill.

Where are the dandelions? my mother asked at the top of the hill. Every summer our backyard blazed yellow with dandelions. I couldn't tell her where they were now.

I turned east on the next street and headed toward the bay. She caught up and I held her hand, which was soft like medicated Kleenex.

Something is following us, she said.

It was the dog from the park, one of my father's hunting dogs, his favorite hunting dog.

Do you remember his name? my mother asked.

Red, I said, though the dog was gray and white.

I could see my father in our backyard throwing a stick high up in the air. He threw the stick higher and higher each time and the gray dog jumped and caught the stick in his jaws. The next winter the dog froze to death in our garage, while we ate sugar cookies and drank warm things in the kitchen at my grandpa's house, not knowing that the temperature had plunged to forty below. The wood heat of the small house was dry, we teased each other, my grandpa laughed even though he didn't know what we were saying.

The dog kennel was empty for a month and then another dog appeared who was tan and my father named him Blackie.

As I walked with my mother, we passed a phone booth without a phone. We passed a bakery without any bread or pastries in the window, though we could smell yeasty dough rising somewhere. We stared into the bakery, and finally an old man leaned out from one of the second-story windows. He was wearing a white apron.

Are you hungry? he asked.

My mother said she was hungry.

No dogs, the man said.

The inside of the man's house was like an art gallery, wooden floors, white walls, tall windows that looked out on a garden of raspberry bushes and ivy. My mother and I sat at the table and put our hands in our laps. A plate of scones appeared. My mother and the man talked about their aging bodies, they talked about the new smells and sounds their bodies made, earthy and yeasty and creaky. They talked about what they used to do. The man had run the bakery for fifty years and my mother had baked for all her children, and then grandchildren, she said, to my surprise, for what seemed like forever. Then she laughed and the golden caps on her molars lit up and she was a star.

My mother and I walked south again, believing we were walking toward the Bay. We talked about the past, and then we talked about the present, and then we talked about the future. We talked about the funeral my mother wanted to have, the color of the casket, the walleye we had engraved on my father's stone. I expected my mother would want a square dancer or the Lord's Prayer. She had been a great dancer and a great prayer, though only praying was left. She said, No, a bird. Just then a pigeon flew over our heads and landed five feet away on the sidewalk, which is not so remarkable given all the pigeons in that part of the City. The dog lunged for it, caught it in his jaws and swallowed it whole.

The light was changing now, fewer clouds, or they had spread out. The sidewalks glistened and my mother's skin grew translucent—I could see thin blue lines in her face, neck and the backs of her hands. The blood was pressing its way toward her heart and then setting out for the arduous trek to her extremities.

As we approached the Bay, more and more weeds grew up through the sidewalk cracks. The damp air, the smell of water and salt. My mother grew tired. I could see the glow in her face dim and her cheeks began to sag again, the way they did when she was done flying in the driveway. She bent over and propped herself on her thighs. I bent over and propped myself on my thighs.

Then she sat down on the sidewalk and lay back on the concrete. I put my jacket under her head. I lay down next to her and the dog lay at my side. I could feel my mother's hip pressed against my hip and my mother's shoulder pressed against my shoulder. I could feel the dog's warm torso against my side; it laid one paw on my hip and thumped its tail, having no idea.

The sidewalk was not uncomfortable, the heat of the concrete, the hardness. But I had no pillow and soon my head began to ache.

I can't feel the back of my head, I said.

But my mother had fallen asleep. And the dog also was sleeping.

I felt obligated to remain still. I imagined the back of my head had opened, that my brain had direct access to the earth. I could hear its deep murmurings, its creaking. I could feel the roots of trees, the maneuverings of underground animals, worms and rodents. I could feel the matrix of the sewage system, metal pipes and underground concrete tunnels, the earth's deep core and the trickling of the water table.

The dog woke and began licking my face, and then my mother's face. Now her face's stroke side was really drooping. We stood up, and the blood dropped into our legs again, and our feet remembered how to hold the weight of our bodies. My mother walked with a limp.

Are we almost there? she asked.

Yes, I said, though I didn't know where there was.

We walked past a row of turquoise, green, and yellow houses, and then down a hill, and there was the Bay glimmering and glimmering in the golden sun like a thousand gold teeth. My mother couldn't walk, so I picked her up and carried her down the hill to a bench near the water's shore. We sat through the three phases of dusk: the blue, the purple, and the black. We sat through the night and the three phases of dawn: the gray, the pink, and the yellow. In the morning I walked home alone through the outskirts of the City. In my small kitchen I fried an egg and then I ate the egg. I turned on the lights, and then I turned off the lights.

THE COAST OF PERU

The calcium in our bones comes from the core of a star. Michelle used to talk a lot about solar systems. She'd lay her books out on the floor and show me pictures. Stars that measured ten times bigger than our sun, supernovas and the rubbery effect of black holes, theories about infinite compression, the birth of hydrogen, lithium, deuterium, and helium. One time she told me that if the earth slipped out of its orbit even for a nanosecond, the oceans would roil and soon we'd be swimming in our apartments like clothed fish. Another time she explained about the galaxies beyond the Milky Way, the colors to be found there, deeper than we could fathom, so deep, she said, that in looking at them one would feel a lasting satisfaction. And she took my hand. She knew for certain that when we die we become those colors, our own planetary nebulas burning red and green and orange.

The best month of her life, she liked to say, was spent in a cave on the southern coast of Peru. Every day she walked the beach to the village and then walked back and cooked a fish over a fire. Sometimes she was so lonely she couldn't breathe unless she sat on a particular boulder near the shore. And yet she stayed until the loneliness became her porch, from which she watched the horizon. At night she sat and listened to the Pacific Ocean chant its leafy litany and the trees howl in the high winds.

On her twenty-fourth birthday, she became solemn and told me that most of the universe was still cold, empty space.

Someday there will be no galaxies. Someday there will be only black holes becoming white holes, white light and infinite suns. And then we will start all over again, Michelle, with floors to sweep, cups to put away in the cupboard, dishes to wash, and dust floating down onto our new dust. Our bones again filled with stars.

THE STARTUP

Today, Larissa is at work, and I am home in our bed supposedly immobilized by a head cold. I lie in bed with pillows under my knees and head, the blankets pulled high over my face. I pretend I am dying, something Michelle and I used to do when we skipped work, and even though her death was nothing like our rehearsals, I think she'd appreciate my use of what my girlfriend calls a therapeutic reboot. First, at dawn when Larissa left, I had a brain tumor; by the time the sun hit the bedroom window I had another form of cancer; and now I am just cradled in an indeterminate coma, in which I am at peace and being nursed by a lot of morphine. I am expended. Gigantic green trees are canopied above my bed.

It is still early morning but Larissa has already texted twice. I didn't respond. I tried to imagine getting out of bed, but all I can imagine is being dead.

Two years ago, Larissa founded a startup company along with two other tech entrepreneurs who live in the Midwest. My adjunct teaching position had been deleted, so Larissa hired me as their user experience person (an *n* of one), researcher, and pseudo-code writer, though as a non-techy English teacher I prefer to be called a translator: I read their code and then recode it back into English. Since the startup, neither Larissa nor I have stayed home from work for even one day, or walked out our front door past 8:00 a.m., or forsaken our Mac Airs for lunch.

An hour after her text, Larissa called and said, in a completely different tone, more wistful than accusing, that she wished she had a cold and could stay home in bed and die too, because she knows that's what I am doing. I asked her if she thought I was being self-indulgent and she said, "Well, yes." Most people don't play dead just to get out of meetings. What Larissa doesn't understand, or has forgotten in her devotion to our mission, is that like any other venture, death features its own risks and responsibilities.

"You're right," I told her, though I have not populated all the required fields, I am being self-indulgent. "But," I said, "I am solving a lot of vital recoding problems while lying in bed." She laughed her new, anxious laugh and said, "You'd better be."

———

There is a bird I have never heard before outside in the rubber tree. Its song is three notes, three notes and then the bird flies to another tree and pauses before it spreads its song into that new space. The wind in the leaves of the eucalyptus makes an ocean-like bass line, low and watery, into my open window and door to the porch. At 11:00 a.m. the mail slides through our slot in the door—so this is when mail arrives!—and the dog barks and barks, until I say thank you, and then she hurtles her fifteen-pound mutt body onto the bed and lies with her snout on my chest, staring at me suspiciously, or in disbelief, waiting for me to get up. I text the dog walker, *No walks today*, and am thankful Larissa opened the door to our porch, which leads to our backyard, before leaving for work. No disturbances.

What air have we to breathe like sea, I think, weirdly. And then I shut my eyes and imagine my muscles and bones, starting with my toes and finally reaching the dura mater around my brain, spreading into the mattress. The green canopy has vanished and now behind the darkness of my eyelids pops up a skeleton riding a bicycle, like a Mexican Día de los Muertos figurine; she waves and her straw hair and her arm bones rattle. Then, in from the periphery, as if my eyelids are a stage, looms a skull with Larissa's red hair and square green glasses, her ivory finger bones linked to a laptop that smolders and then emits strands of black computer code, braided like DNA, unraveling, faster and faster, individual symbols breaking free, morphing into an arabesque of tiny black birds.

———

At noon, Larissa calls again. I can hear the grinding of the printer in her closet-sized office and further off the hyena whine of our shared scanner. But she doesn't say anything; she just breathes and sighs, which is unusual for Larissa. Today, from 5:15 to 5:45 p.m., she will pitch to a venture capitalist visiting the City from one of the most *vital* firms on the peninsula, *vital* being one of Larissa's favorite words, which makes me like her. And though my role is to be purely supportive, plumping out our small round vintage table and looking the capitalist in the eye, at the ready, while Larissa PowerPoints (a presentation I made for her last week), I feel sorry, though not sorry enough, that she has to do it alone.

"It's almost lunch," I say, mustering my best imitation of Larissa's cheerleader voice. "You can you can," I say.

Six months ago, the heroic hours that we had both loved, and to which Larissa and the other twenty-eight-year-old techs are accustomed, began to overload my thirty-five-year-old system. That is my conjecture. Sometimes, after the fog burns off through the one office window, and the sun barges onto our common-space rug, I stutter out and crash belly down on the warm fibers. Within a few minutes, Larissa crouches at my side. *You can you can*, she whispers through my hair into my ear, until I drag myself up and slog back to my desk chair.

Larissa builds possibilities with symbols. Asterisks and parens are secret messages to the gods behind the screen. I build bridges between that secret world and those of us who live outside the screen; people Larissa calls the RTFMers (read the fucking manual). And when I think I cannot go on, I dream into the life Larissa and I will create when the startup goes public and changes the world, especially our world. For our first trip, which we have already researched, we will hike through southern Mexico and sleep in hammocks. I will show Larissa the tomb of the unknown skeleton in the Zapotec region, where Michelle and I got stranded and huddled all night under a twelve-foot-high stone carving of Cocijo, the Zapotec rain god.

But, lately, I cannot imagine going anywhere. My imagination circuits have been injected with Novocain. And I am beginning to think there will be no end, that Larissa has turned into a startup zombie; when this one sails forth she will just want to build another. Last week we met with some other entrepreneurs about their ideas, came home at two o'clock in the morning, and on our way to the bedroom fell asleep on the rug in the living room fully clothed, our jackets halfway off one arm, like the people you see in parks, sleeping off a binge. At dawn, I found Larissa bolt upright against the sofa, staring at a stain shaped like a crescent moon on the carpet. "I can't feel anything," she said, her face pale. But then, before I had fully awakened and without changing her clothes, she walked out of our front door and west toward Capp Street to work.

——————

What Larissa doesn't know is that while I lie nose down on the office rug, and here in my bed, I think about Michelle, something I haven't done much for the past three years. I think of Michelle's deadness as an open parenthesis—most of the data has vanished: the way her hands felt on my face, the smell of her skin and hair, what she loved or didn't love. I shut my eyes and try to conjure her face, but instead Cocijo's face flashes past, his wide, blunt nose, his long, forked, serpent-like tongue. For a moment my pulse drops—not grief, but the absence of grief like a missing rib. The absence even of the memory of grief.

You said you would never forget me, Michelle says now, black boots kicked back on the chair she dragged in from the kitchen, over the wood floors the way Larissa would never do. She leans back and smiles at me, her own cheeks fatter and more relaxed than in photographs. "What are you eating?" I ask. She opens her mouth and on her tongue floats one white petal. There we are in the park on a blanket in the rhododendron grove, gazing at the flowered boughs, dying and oblivious to the industry of the world outside our view.

"Do you miss me?" I ask, and she sadly shakes her head no.

Michelle disappears and I hear wind tunneling through the apartment, even though the back windows are closed. Where are you now, my long-gone Michelle? And where is the memory I used to be?

The dog, who has crept up to the head of our bed, is padding around on the edge of my pillow, nesting, next to my head. Her fur smells like corn, and her paws smell like fried cornbread topped with salt. She presses her back against my cheek and I press my nose into her.

"*Bi'cu'*," I say. It means "dog" in Zapotec.

"Bi'cu'," I say again, but the dog could not care less.

In the Zapotec tomb a bone carving of a little dog, ancestor of the Chihuahua, sat perched on a shelf next to an urn. The human skeleton, assumedly the dog's master, was loaded with gold, amber, turquoise, silver, alabaster. In other burial sites the archeologists found actual skeletons of dogs. One wore a collar made of jade beads and its ears were plugged with turquoise; from its ankles dangled bracelets with little bells of pure gold.

Something weird happens—suddenly I miss the smell of my dog's fur. But here I am on my bed listening to the bird and wind with the bi'cu' right here at my face. I am mourning her smell even while buried in it.

I sit up in bed and wipe my eyes. 3:00 p.m. Two hours before Larissa shakes hands with our potential financial angel. I raise my head to see my jacket and shoes on the floor beside the pile of laundry, but that's as far as I get. I lie back down. *This is the end,* I think. Suddenly I know that the two sides of death are the same; Larissa and the dog die to me, I die to them.

At first I feel afraid, but then I feel nothing.

———

"What will you do when I am gone?" I ask Larissa the next time she calls.

"Where are you going?" she asks, and then she says, "Oh."

She is chewing something simultaneously soft and crunchy (a Clif Bar?), which means she is not having a good day. If it were a good day she would have stuffed down a sandwich delivered from the deli down the street, and that would have lasted her until dinner. She stops chewing, and I can hear the rusty whine of her bottom desk drawer opening. More chewing. She has accomplished figuring out one thing and is about to figure out another, which is what she does all day. Today she has to figure out the promises she can make to the venture capitalist, while convincing him of the fifty-two ways they'll profit from our faithful labor. When laypeople ask us exactly what we are starting up, Larissa says, "Well, we are figuring that out." I say nothing. I play dumb.

Larissa and I want to link people to their vocational dreams (Larissa worked for a year as a school counselor), but we fear someone else will link to dreams before us. For example, if you dream of being a marine biologist, our application, which features filmed interviews with people who have achieved their dreams, should give you a comprehensive picture of what your life would look like: How did they get there? What do they find most rewarding? Please depict a typical day of work. Etc.

For the low-fidelity prototype, the codes will be set to meet 1,075 vocational dreams (don't ask me how they came up with that number). With enough money, Larissa and her buddies hope to reach a million dreams. (Work. Work. Work.) Our dream—though I am starting to think Larissa has another— is to make enough money to walk around places saying hello to people in their own languages, maybe even start a school. We will read the books we want, and lie in bed every morning listening to birds and wind and traffic. And even though I know the risk of going backward to who I was with Michelle, I can't help asking—which moments matter?

On the next phone call with Larissa I say, "I want you to promise that you will go on without me."

"No, you don't," she says.

"No, I mean it. I don't want you to be alone."

"Yes you do," she says, but not unkindly. "You want me to be alone forever, you want me to hack off my hair, shred my clothes and pitch myself onto your casket. You want me to supplicate in deserts and moan into the sea, to stumble the wind-barren plains, thirsty and bereft, blinding eternity with your name. Just like Michelle wanted you to do for her."

To that soliloquy, I don't know what to say.

She's right. We give up our dead too easily; Michelle nods in agreement. She's looking imperiously at me now from her perch on my clothes dresser (which really is like Michelle). She has dyed her hair pitch black (or was it always that black?) and over her jeans shimmers a satin robe the color of the vintage titanium PowerBook.

"We need toilet paper," Larissa says. "And fruit for breakfast. Maybe in your afterlife you'll shop, OK?"

As we hiked toward the tomb of the unknown skeleton, I leaned on Michelle's shoulder and we ascended into the thinnest air we had ever breathed, our oxygen-depleted brains painting the rusty ground bright orange and the cacti a fluorescent green. At the top, we rambled up and down the pyramids in a semi-hallucinatory gleam, but when we returned to the entrance the sky had dulled the air gray. All the buses were gone and they weren't coming back. We walked out to the road. Empty. Where had the people gone? And then—it seemed so sudden—the screen dropped black, and the road and parking lot vanished. A wind tossed dirt into our hair and eyes, thunder, then lightning—and then rain pushed us toward a skinny brush-lined path we hadn't seen before. A low stone ledge led to an antechamber, a tiny alley, ending at a closed tomb door. We crouched against it, and through the rain and wind the cold stone face of Cocijo, holding his bucket of water and bolt of lightning, stared down at us. Sometime in the middle of the night the sky cleared and the traffic of the stars shot across the black, flying the dead and all their jewels to their ancestors in heaven.

At least that is my retrieval—the artifact of the day.

I wake to a lung sound. One of us, the dog or I, is wheezing. The green hill of the inhale, the emptiness at the top, the valley as the breath tumbles down into emptiness again. In the dim room we listen to this breathing.

Rolling over the buildings and trees, the fog is in from the ocean like a wet gray cloud. I can feel early evening even before I lift my head from the pillow and see it out the window. The lavender, which Larissa placed on the table next to my bed this morning, sends out a sweet scent. Tomorrow, the fog will accompany us to work again, and by ten o'clock will burn off, the sun brightening the red common-space rug. The trains will chug down Church Street and the Muni buses slide through the glittering sheet of blue sky, the sky always blue though we rarely see it anymore, and the blue always windy, and for those fifteen minutes when I walk to and from work the god of wind bears me down even when I wear my hat past my eyebrows.

"Our app could really help people," Larissa says when she calls at 4:15 p.m. "I know," I say, and part of me still believes it. But I don't know what else to say. "I'm sorry," I say. And I am sorry. At 5:00 p.m. I imagine Larissa at the small conference table in the corner of the room, sitting cross-legged on the plastic vintage chair, her green designer glasses pushed close to her nose, her Mac Air poised. She will have to tell herself to look away from the screen, to look the man in the eye, to pause between sentences, to remember that he may not speak her language and so she will have to translate—to recode her code—without too many details. I will not be there to remind her.

I realize I may really be losing Larissa. She will stay in the land of high-wire synaptic exuberance, the clicking of finger-nails on the keypad, the wild hum of the focused, charging mind. Why are the places we feel most alive so deadly?

I sit up and watch the fog merge with the building next door, and then the evening coolness bristles the hair on my arms. The neighbor is outside on the sidewalk, talking to his children who are young and say they want to be veterinarians, and then a bit later I hear him start his car. The evening rush hour traffic on Waller Street is steady but not bustling; it's as if they had rehearsed it, just as the sound of one car fades another approaches from Haight Street or Duboce.

We got the money, she texts me at 6:00 p.m. No happy face, no exclamation points. Five minutes later she texts, *Now we are really and truly fucked.*

The floor has begun to darken with shadows.

After the early Zapotecs abandoned Monte Albán, somewhere between 700 and 950 CE, the Mixtec moved in, remodeled, and thus destroyed a lot of Zapotec artifacts. But researchers do know that after the rains the Zapotec fed Cocijo the fresh blood of sacrificial infants, children, dogs, commoners, and captives. A thanksgiving. The cult of the dead. The people who die of disease and old age get to travel in company bearing gifts to paradise, but those who die in sudden violent deaths, like the bicycle accident that crushed Michelle's frontal lobe, don't travel anywhere.

The Zapotecs believed that anything that moved—smoke, wind, rain, the steam off a cup of coffee—was alive and anything that did not move was dead. I push the covers back and get out of bed.

From the top of my dresser I gather a pair of earrings Larissa made me from integrated circuits woven with strands of her red hair. I dig out from the top drawer a fake pearl necklace from Michelle, from the laundry my favorite T-shirt, and from the bottom of the hallway closet a scarf my mother sent from the cold northern region before she understood my new climate. I climb back into bed with my loot and array my gems around me, the earrings near my cheek and the necklace at my feet. The dog settles into the crook of my arm.

The morning after our trek to Monte Albán, a run-down pickup returned us to the city, dropped us off right outside our hotel, a shabby beautiful building with turquoise hallways and scrubbed orange brick floors. We slept all through the day and that night, until Julio, the manager whose three children read superhero comic books in the lounge, knocked at our door. *Señoritas, están bien? Por favor, no se mueren aquí.*

Todo está muy bien, we said. *Señor, no se preocupe. Somos tan alegre.* We were so happy.

This is how you say *Everything is OK* in five different languages.

———

I hear the door open, the soft brush of the frame against our hall rug, and then close. I hear a sigh and a thump of shoes tossed off in the hallway. Not even seven o'clock. I can't remember the last time Larissa came home this early.

Her hair, long and red as the day we met, smells like carpet fibers. She's been lying on the rug in the common space. She lifts up the covers and climbs into bed beside me, curling her legs around mine.

We take each other's hands under the covers. "Wherever you're going, I'm going with you," she says.

And I am so afraid and so awake.

ACKNOWLEDGMENTS

Thank you to the editors of the following journals for publishing stories from *The Fifth Woman*, some in earlier versions or with different titles: "A Hat Shaped Like a Dog That Looked Like a Cat," *Arroyo Literary Review*; "Two Clean Things," "The Dog," and "The Phone Call," *Black Warrior Review*; "The Party" (as "Frontiers") and "The Ravine," *Cimarron Review*; "The Letter" (as "On the Roof"), *Epoch*; "Ants," *Glimmer Train*; "The Horse," *Glimmer Train Writer's Bulletin*; "The Crack," "The Fifth Woman" (as "A Fifth Woman"), and "A Pair of Sunfish," *Green Mountains Review*; and "Reception," *The Kenyon Review*.

"Frontiers," now titled "The Party," was named a distinguished story of 2015 in *The Best American Short Stories 2016*, edited by Junot Díaz. Thank you.

This book grew from the care, intelligence, and collaborative spirit of Ann Pelletier, Jesse Nissim, and Barbara Tomash. What a blessing to be accompanied by their goodwill and honesty. Cathy Rose, thank you for the writing retreats and for reading drafts. And thank you to Toni Graham for reading my work for twenty-five years. Thanks also to Rebekah Pickard and Rebecca Haseltine for listening, reading, and providing feedback.

I thank the studio apartment, red writing table, and window that looked out over a small street and a four-story apartment building in the Mission neighborhood of San Francisco. And all the animate and inanimate beings in the world. Especially Edgar.

Thank you to Samantha Hunt for writing the story "Three Days" (*The New Yorker*, January 16, 2006), which inspired me to write "The Horse."

In "Ants" the narrator is reading from *Autobiography of Red* by Anne Carson.

I am deeply grateful to Sarabande Books for their years of publishing meaningful literature, and special thanks to Kristen Miller for her brilliant editing. Big thanks to Stacey D'Erasmo!

SARABANDE BOOKS is a nonprofit literary press located in Louisville, KY. Founded in 1994 to champion poetry, short fiction, and essay, we are committed to creating lasting editions that honor exceptional writing. For more information, please visit sarabandebooks.org.